MURDER
at the
BIG HOUSE

by

W.A. Patterson

W.A. Patterson

Murder at the Big House

ISBN-13: 978-1726068475
ISBN-10: 1726068471

W.A. Patterson

W.A. Patterson

CHAPTER 1

'What's that in your mouth?'

The stocky little terrier adopted a defiant stance and locked eyes with his mistress. His tail stood erect and he wagged it slowly in anticipation, daring her to try and take the object he held between his jaws.

'Ya little divil, those are me knickers! Una reached for her item of freshly-laundered smalls but he was too quick for her.

'Spit 'em out!' she yelled, as she chased him around the kitchen table in what had become an all-too-familiar ritual. Occasionally he would pause, allowing her come closer, only to leap out of reach just as she thought she had him. Finally, exhausted, Una plopped down onto a kitchen chair.

'Ah, keep 'em,' she said, 'I don't care. I'm going out for a *walk*.' She emphasised the last word and blessed herself, just in case lying to a dog constituted a sin. He scampered over and threw himself onto his back at her feet. When she reached down to grab the undergarment in his mouth his jaws opened gently, releasing his spoils into her hand. She rewarded him by giving his belly a scratch.

'Lucky for you you're cute,' she told him, 'otherwise you'd have been out that door long ago.'

He jumped into her lap and began lathering her face with his tongue. Una tried to push him away but all attempts to fend him off were futile.

'Alright so,' she said, 'c'mere to me fer a cuddle.' She threw her arms around the little dog and pulled him to her, covering his head with noisy kisses. He surrendered to the welcome attention.

Before Aine had left to attend law school in Dublin, she presented her grandmother with a three-month-old Cairn Terrier. 'So you won't be lonely in the house on your own,' she'd told her. Una had been far from happy with her granddaughter's gesture but, no matter how hard she'd tried to dislike the little dog, the truth was that he'd not only filled her house to overflowing, but her heart too.

She looked down into his bright eyes and he gave her the nearest thing to a smile a dog can, his pink tongue barely protruding from his mouth.

'You're an aul' flea bag,' she told him, 'but somehow, God help me, you've wheedled your way into my affections.' Just then the phone rang. 'G'way now.' She pushed the dog gently off her lap onto the floor, then hauled herself to her feet. She removed the receiver from a phone on the wall.

'Hello?'

'Is that Mrs. Murphy?'

'Una Murphy speaking. Who is this?' The man's voice was vaguely familiar but she couldn't quite place it.

'It's Terrence. Terrence McCarthy. Remember me?'

'Monsignor McCarthy, I do o'course. Well, how's things?' It was a commonly-used Irish greeting and, as such, did not require a response.

'Listen, I know this is out of the blue but I wondered if I could come and have a chat with you and Mrs. Cahill. There's something I need your help with.'

Una couldn't imagine what help two elderly women could be to a senior priest but she owed Terrence McCarthy a debt of gratitude. After all, it was thanks to his influence that Aine had secured a place at Trinity Law School. He'd also been instrumental in solving the bog body case.

'No problem. When would you like to come over?'

'As a matter of fact, I'm parked outside right now. I'm heading for your front door as I speak.'

'I'll put the kettle on so. Give me a minute though, I just have to put the dog out the back. He behaves like a thing demented if anyone other than Joan comes to the house. I'll be right with you.'

The terrier was acutely aware that a visitor's arrival was imminent and no power on earth would convince him to be exiled to the back garden. After chasing him around the kitchen table several times, Una gave up. She shook her finger at him.

'Alright, you can stay, but you'd better not go making a holy show o' me!'

She made her way through the hallway and he followed her. When she pulled open the front door, she was surprised to find the priest dressed in casual attire. He looked considerably less intimidating than he had in his priestly robes.

Before she had a chance to welcome him, the dog ran out from behind her and hurled himself at the newcomer. Terrence staggered backwards and laughed.

'Hello, little fella! You look just like Toto from the Wizard of Oz.'

'Toto, is it?' exclaimed Una, trying to gain control of Finn who, in an attempt to garner the unbridled attention of his new playmate, was now launching himself off the floor at repeated intervals. 'More like one of those infernal flying monkeys!'

'What's his name?'

'Finn McCool, my granddaughter's idea.' Una made a grab for the terrier's collar but he dodged her. 'Suits him, the elusive little hell-raiser.'

'I gather Finn McCool is a stranger to training classes.'

'Not exactly. I did take him but he was expelled after the first lesson. Too disruptive they said.'

'Have you considered exorcism?' The priest was still laughing. 'I could perform one for you.'

'Ah sure if you took the divil out of him, all I'd have left is a scruffy ball of fur.' Una made a final lunge and managed to hook a finger under the little dog's collar. Bent double, she led him back into the hallway and waved the priest inside. Come in, Monsignor. Go through to the parlour, you know where it is. I'll be back in a minute with some tea. Mind your shoelaces by the way! Finn likes to eat them.'

Una got to work in the kitchen and within minutes was carrying a tray into the parlour. A dark brown spout and handle peeked out from either end of a knitted tea cosy, blue and white cups rattled in their matching saucers and a pile of chocolate digestive biscuits conspired to slide off their plate en masse. She was surprised to see Finn lying on the priest's lap as if the pair had been friends for years. Terrence was scratching behind the dog's ears and Finn was lapping up the attention.

'Did his batteries finally wear out?'

'No, he ran out of shoelaces.' Terrence clicked his shoes together to emphasise the point and Una looked down. Bits of chewed-off shoestring lay strewn on the carpet around his feet, like so many black worms.

'I did warn you.'

'Don't worry, they're old shoes.' Una could see they were no such thing and that the priest was being magnanimous.

'I'm assuming this isn't a social visit,' she said. The smile slid from his handsome face.

'I'm afraid not. I'll explain, but I was hoping Mrs. Cahill would be here too.'

'Oh don't worry about that, she'll be here. Joan doesn't miss much. I expect she's touching up her hair and make-up.'

The words had barely escaped Una's lips when they heard the front door open, then click shut. When Joan entered the room Finn looked up, then put his head back on the priest's lap.

Joan shot the animal a look of disdain. She didn't like dogs much. She made an exception when it came to corgis on account of their royal connection, foxhounds too because her late husband had been a member of the hunt club when they lived in England. However, this scruffy specimen clearly didn't fall into either of those two noble categories.

'Really, my dear, I do wish you'd lock that thing outside when visitors come. I'm sure your gentleman caller doesn't want to go home reeking of dog.' Una ignored her friend's remark and made the necessary introductions.

'The Monsignor would like our help,' she told Joan. 'I don't know what with yet, more skulduggery involving the Church probably.'

A smile flashed across the priest's face and was gone. 'You could never be accused of mincing your words, Mrs. Murphy.' Una caught a southern inflection in his practiced upper-class Irish accent that she hadn't noticed before.

'Is that a slight Cork accent I detect?'

He nodded. 'I was born and raised in Kinsale.'

'Really?' Joan was surprised. 'You don't sound like any Cork man I've ever met. I can understand what you're saying for one thing.'

He laughed. 'Would ya loike me ta talk in me native accent?'

'God no,' exclaimed Una, raising her hands in mock indignation. 'Spare us. Now, what's the story?'

The priest's expression became sombre. 'It's a personal matter. My aunt died a week ago.'

'I'm very sorry for your loss. Was she old?'

'Oh yes, she was quite old.'

Una glanced at Joan. 'Well it's not unusual for old people to die, Monsignor.'

'Indeed, but her housekeeper died the next day. She was only in her mid-forties.'

'What have the Gardaí to say about it?'

'The Coroner's report states both died of natural causes. The Gardaí have concluded it was an unfortunate coincidence.'

Una leaned forward in her chair. 'But you don't agree.'

'I'm convinced there's more to it. Aunt Geraldine was in excellent health and so was Lelia, but I've hit a brick wall. There were no signs of foul play and both toxicology reports came back negative. They're saying my aunt died of respiratory failure and that her housekeeper died from a heart arrhythmia... ventricular fibrillation.'

Una sipped her tea and watched Terrence with narrowed eyes. 'Let's say the deaths are suspicious,' she said, 'just for argument's sake. What motive could there be?'

'My aunt was a very wealthy woman, Mrs. Murphy. Perhaps you've heard of Lady Geraldine Hennessy of Moonbeg Manor. She was my father's sister. Her estate is near Fethard, not far from here.'

'Of course!' exclaimed Joan. The aristocracy was involved and suddenly her interest in the matter had escalated. 'I didn't realise Lady Geraldine was your aunt! I heard she passed away on Tipp FM's death notices. I'm very sorry, Monsignor.'

She turned to Una. 'My dear, Moonbeg Manor is a magnificent house by all accounts!'

'It's one of the finest historic mansions in Ireland.' There was nothing boastful in the priest's manner, he was merely stating a fact. 'The land belonging to it covers over eight hundred acres, some of the most fertile farmland in the country. Since her husband passed away ten years ago, my aunt has been leasing out the land. She was a woman of considerable means.'

'And tell us,' said Una, 'who stands to inherit your aunt's fortune?'

'Geraldine and her husband didn't have children of their own, so the estate would be split between my aunt's niece and nephews.'

'You being one of the nephews.'

Terrence sensed the direction in which Una's train of thought was heading.

'I'm heir to our own family seat in Kinsale. Our estate will come to me when my mother passes so I have no need of my aunt's money. In fact I've already expressed a wish that Moonbeg Manor be given over to An Taisce.'

'What's that?' asked Joan. 'I'm not familiar with it.'

'It's like your National Trust,' explained Una. 'It's a heritage organisation.'

'I see. Tell me, Monsignor, where are the others beneficiaries you mentioned?'

'My cousins? They're out of the picture, Mrs. Cahill. They live in South Africa, it's where they were born. I've only met them a handful of times.'

'So why have you come to us?' asked Una. 'What is it you want?'

'I want the truth, Mrs. Murphy, the same thing you wanted when that poor woman's body was found in the bog outside Ballyanny.'

'But how can we can help?'

'The police aren't interested in delving any further. As far as they're concerned the two deaths were a tragic coincidence so the case is closed. What I'd like is for you two ladies to come and stay with me at Moonbeg Manor. I thought if we could spend time there, we'd have a chance to look around, ask questions without arousing suspicion.'

'How would you explain having two strangers in tow?'

Terrence lifted the dog off his lap and leaned forward in his armchair. 'I've been thinking about that. There was no love lost between our two families. My father wouldn't even speak to Geraldine after she married William Hennessy. My mother kept in touch for a time, she even came up to Moonbeg once or twice, but then my father found out and put a stop to it. After he died, my mother didn't want to go against his wishes. She hasn't set foot inside Moonbeg Manor for twenty years or more. I doubt if any of the staff would know her now. I thought perhaps one of you could play the role of my mother.'

Una puckered her forehead. 'It's an idea,' she said, 'but a dangerous one. There's always a chance someone will remember your mother and even if they don't, one of us could slip up, use the wrong name. Then the whole jig would be up.' She pondered for a moment. 'Has your mother any sisters?'

'She has one, my Aunt Brigid. Why?'

'Are the members of staff at Moonbeg familiar with Brigid?'

'No, they don't know my mother's family at all.'

'Then I suggest the part to be played is that of your mother's sister. That way we could use our own names and the chance of inadvertently giving ourselves away would be reduced.'

'Altogether a better idea,' agreed Terrence. 'You're really rather good at this sort of thing aren't you, Mrs. Murphy.'

'Ah Joan and I are experts when it comes to subterfuge. After all, we've spent years studying it.'

'You have?'

'Of course. We've read everything Agatha Christie wrote on the art of deception.'

Joan raised her hand like a pupil who needed the bathroom. 'Can I be the aunt?'

Terrence smiled. 'I appreciate your enthusiasm, Mrs. Cahill, but I'm afraid the role would be wholly unsuited to you.'

'Oh.' Joan's expression was one of disappointment. 'Don't you consider me suitably refined?'

'Quite the reverse. You're far too refined to be a member of my mother's family. Mrs. Murphy would be much better suited to the part.'

'I beg yer pardon?' snapped Una.

Terrence had dug himself a hole and now he began to wallpaper it. 'I didn't mean to offend you, it's just that my mother's people are known for their.... candour.'

'If you didn't want to offend me, it's too late! And I take it that by candour you mean they have a surly manner about them.'

'Well they do, that's true, but what I mean is they're frank and honest. They speak their mind.' Beads of sweat began to break out on the priest's forehead.

'Oh you're perfect for the part,' gushed Joan, 'just as the Monsignor said.'

'Please say you'll help me, Una,' he implored. 'You are the first person I thought of when I decided to investigate my aunt's death. If anyone can get to the bottom of it, it's you and Joan.'

She cast him a sideways glance. His eyes beseeched her to help him.

'Alright,' she grinned. 'If you put it that way, how could we refuse?'

Finn didn't have a clue what was going on but he knew his mistress was excited about something and he barked his approval.

CHAPTER 2

'We'll need some background information if we're going to pull this off,' said Una. 'Tell us about your mother, Terrence. It'll give me a better idea of how her sister might conduct herself.'

The priest sat back in his armchair and sighed. 'Well now, let's see.' He pressed his fingertips together to form the shape of a church steeple, the irony of which wasn't lost on Una, and studied the ceiling for a moment. 'She's a very strong-minded woman, my mother. Straight-talking, the type who doesn't suffer fools gladly.'

'There you are, Una!' exclaimed Joan. 'That's you to a tee!'

'What's that supposed to mean? I'm a gobby auld biddy, am I?'

'I said no such thing,' protested Joan.

'That's what you meant!'

'I did not. I just meant that you....' Joan struggled to think of something that wouldn't offend her friend, '...you call a spade a spade.' Una's face was still red with indignation so Joan battled on bravely. 'You're the strong, outspoken one out of the two of us, I'd be far too nervous to play the part.' Una's complexion had begun to return to its normal colour and Joan should have stopped there but, flushed with success, she continued on. 'You're versatile too. You'll have no trouble pretending to be something you're not.'

'Oh so now it's a charlatan I am, is it? A wolf in sheep's clothing!'

The priest had been following the conversation, looking back and forth between the two women as if he was in the front row of a Wimbledon singles final. He decided he'd better intervene before the match turned into all out war. In the absence of a white flag, he held up his hands in surrender.

'Ladies! Ladies, please! I expected better behaviour from two mature....'

'Jayzus, now I'm old! I don't know why ye don't just put me in a home and be done with it!' Una's thick neck bulged and Terrence watched in amazement as her face slowly turned the colour of an artificial violet on the table beside her.

'Did I say old?' He had been drawn involuntarily into the fray. 'I said mature, as in experienced.'

Una grunted. 'I might have known you'd take her side. You snobs always stick together.'

'Think about it this way. If you play the part of my aunt, then Mrs. Cahill could be your lady's companion, your.... subordinate.'

Una's face lit up. 'I like the sound of that. So I'd be her boss?'

'In effect, yes'

'Well in that case, I think it's a grand idea.'

'You would,' grumbled Joan, 'now you're playing the lady.'

'So is it settled, Una?' asked Terrence. 'Will you be my aunt?'

'Can I take a wooden spoon to you if you misbehave?'

'You cannot.'

'Can I take a sally rod to your arse if you're bold?'

'I'm afraid I cannot condone violence of any kind,' he smiled, 'I'm a man of peace.'

'Ah sure you take all the fun out of it altogether but alright, I'll play the character.'

'Talking about characters, I should probably warn you about Matty. You'll meet him when we get to Moonbeg.'

'Matty?' said Joan.

'Yes, Matthew McDonnell. His grandfather was a big hurling fan and insisted his grandson be named after Matthew Maher. Maher played for the Tipp senior team back in the day and they nicknamed him Matty. Our Matty is the caretaker at Moonbeg. Well, he's much more than that really, he does just about everything. He's the chauffeur, he looks after the horses, he tends the gardens and he does odd jobs around the house. He's a giant of a man with a heart of gold. Clumsy in word and deed alright, but you won't find a kinder or more genuine being on God's earth. Matty's been with my aunt for years, I was a just a teenager when he started. Many's the time I helped him out in the stables or the garage or in the garden, just so I could listen to his stories.' Terrence laughed. 'He tells the longest, most disjointed stories you've ever heard, but I still love listening to them.'

'What's the matter with him?' asked Una. 'Is he thick?'

'Not at all! People are quick to judge Matty but there's more to him than meets the eye. There's a sharp intellect inside that big skull of his. It's just the day-to-day things he struggles with.'

'Should we put him on our suspect list?'

'Matty?' Terrence laughed. 'Not a chance. He wouldn't hurt a fly. I trust that man with my life.'

'It's not your life I'm concerned with, Monsignor. It's mine and Joan's.' Terrence grinned broadly, not the well-practiced pseudo smile that Una remembered from their previous encounters, but one of genuine affection for a man he clearly held in high esteem.

'There's one more thing you should probably know about him. He'll no doubt be dining with us at Moonbeg, Aunt Geraldine always had him to dinner, so you might as well know that his table manners aren't what you might be accustomed to. He'd eat a bale of hay if you sprinkled sugar on it. He once told me eating makes him hungry.'

'Well thanks for the warning,' said Una, 'I'm sure we'll meet him soon enough. In the meantime, let's get back to your mother. What's her name, by the way?'

'Mary, of course, the same as every other first-born Cork girl.'

'You surprise me. I expected a lady of such standing to have a more... exotic name.'

Joan tittered. 'I think Una was expecting something unusual,' she told Terrence, 'like Concepta perhaps.'

Una snorted. 'Or Beyonce or Madonna, eh Joan?' The two women giggled uncontrollably.

'Private joke?' asked the priest.

'Sorry, Monsignor.' Una wiped her eyes. 'You had to be there to appreciate it. And if you recall, you were always one step behind.'

'Which is why I want you two ladies to be my allies this time, instead of my adversaries.' Finn had resumed his place on the priest's lap and was fast asleep. Dreaming, he growled at some imagined menace.

'It's about time for his walk.' At Una's remark, the little dog woke and jumped down onto the floor.

'Thank the Lord for that,' said Terrence, 'my leg's gone dead.'

'Then a walk will do you good.' Una tossed a brown leather leash to him and he hooked it up to the dog's collar. Finn grabbed the part he could reach in his mouth. 'That's it, boy, take our guest for a walk.' She pulled a small plastic bag from her apron pocket and handed it to the priest. 'Don't bring him back 'til he's taken a dump.'

'I'll do my best,' he laughed.

The door had barely clicked shut when Joan whispered, 'What do you think, my dear?'

'I think we'd better make ourselves a big pot of tea, pet. One cup's not going to be nearly enough for a case of this magnitude.'

*

'Of course it could be just as the police said,' mused Joan, as she sipped her tea. 'It could be merely a tragic coincidence. Stranger things have happened.'

'It could o'course, but then why would Terrence suspect foul play?'

'It's his family, Una. The Monsignor is emotionally involved; we can hardly expect him to be objective.'

'I suppose that's why he needs us.'

'What about those cousins he mentioned in South Africa?'

'What about them? They're six thousand miles away.'

'You hear about contract killings all the time.'

'Well we'll bear them in mind, but I think yer man Matty is someone we should take a long hard look at, despite what Terrence says.'

'Of course Terrence himself could be a suspect, dear. He says he has nothing to gain but what if the motive isn't financial? What if it's personal?'

'That possibility hadn't escaped me either. In fact as it stands, Joanie, you and I are the only ones we can rule out.'

'So where do we start?'

'Like the song says, pet, we start at the very beginning. Whisht! They're coming back.' The dog entered the kitchen first. 'Well, Finn! Did you behave for the nice gentleman?' Terrence followed him in, his previously well-groomed hair windswept.

'I think I can safely pronounce your dog hollow, Mrs. Murphy,' he declared, holding up the bag. 'I'm delighted to report not one, but three dumps. What would you like me to do with this?'

'Keep it as a souvenir if you like.' Una winked at Joan.

Terrence reached down and ruffled the scruffy little dog's head. 'He might look like a toilet brush on legs, but he's a cute little fella alright.'

Finn wagged his tail and rolled over onto his back to have his belly rubbed. The two women watched with interest. The endearing interaction between man and dog pushed Terrence further down the list of suspects, but didn't exclude him from it.

'Tell me about those cousins you mentioned in South Africa,' said Una. 'How do they make their living?'

Terrence pulled up his sleeves and began washing his hands at the kitchen sink.

'Well now, let's see. Johann qualified as a doctor but I think he works at a research facility now. His twin sister is Greta. The last I heard she was working at a university. Poor Greta has suffered with mental health problems over the years.'

'Are either of them married?'

'I know this sounds ridiculous but I don't have a clue what their marital status is. Last time I saw them was at Moonbeg Manor. Aunt Evelyn had brought them over to stay with Aunt Josephine, I suppose they'd have been in their early teens. I haven't set eyes on them since and we don't keep in touch. As you may have gathered, we're not a close-knit family.'

'What's their surname?' It was Joan's turn to ask the questions.

'Van Houten.'

'Is that Afrikaans?'

'No, their father came from the Netherlands. Hans was a mining engineer, or geologist or some such thing. He met my aunt when she was holidaying in Amsterdam.'

'Are the parents still alive?'

'No, Hans has been dead for a while now. Aunt Evelyn died sometime last year. Evelyn was my father's other sister. There were just the three of them, all gone now that Geraldine is dead.'

'What did Hans and Evelyn die of?' asked Una.

'I haven't the slightest idea,' replied Terrence, drying his hands on a kitchen towel. 'As I said, we're not close.'

Una had retrieved a notepad and pen from a drawer. 'It might be helpful if you could find out,' she said, scribbling down some notes. 'See if you can find out what Johann's specialty is too, if he has one, and what Greta's work entails.'

Terrence joined them at the kitchen table. 'Why the interest in the twins? You can't possibly think they're involved.'

'I'm keeping an open mind. After all, the whole thing could turn out to be a wild goose chase, Monsignor, a product of someone's overactive imagination.'

He laughed. 'Do I strike you as the paranoid type, Mrs. Murphy?'

'As a matter of fact you don't, and if I thought this was just paranoia on your part, Joan and I wouldn't be accompanying you to Fethard.'

'Then you agree to help?'

'We already said so, didn't we?'

He grinned. 'Just double-checking you hadn't changed your minds while I was out picking up dog shit.'

CHAPTER 3

'Alright, Joan, let's just suppose there is some validity to the Monsignor's suspicions.'

After making arrangements for their journey to Moonbeg Manor the following morning, Terrence had left and the two friends were able to discuss the matter without having to consider his sensitivities.

'I'm not saying there is villainy at play here, it could just be all in his mind, but let's suspend for now any preconceived notions that rural Ireland is immune from murder most foul.'

'Don't you think you're getting carried away with all this, Una. You're starting to sound like an Agatha Christie novel and real life isn't like that. Just because we uncovered one conspiracy, it doesn't mean we should treat every death as suspicious.'

'Think what the two victims have in common.'

'Alleged victims, dear. We still don't know if any crime has been committed.'

'Alright then, think what the two alleged victims have in common. They're both female, they lived in the same house, they ate the same food and they died within a day of each other. Now that has to be more than coincidence, wouldn't you say?'

'Well no, not necessarily. Look at the differences. One woman was old and rich, the other young and working class. The old lady died in one wing of the house, the housekeeper in another. The toxicology reports showed nothing untoward and both women were officially found to have died of natural causes... different natural causes. Their deaths were untimely, of that there is no doubt, but as far as I'm concerned it's perfectly reasonable to consider them coincidental.'

Una shrugged her shoulders. 'Well if you're so certain there's been no crime committed, you might as well stay at home. I'll go to the big house with the Monsignor while you mind Finn.' The dog heard his name and shot to attention. He looked at Una, rotating his head as far as it would go to one side, the way dogs do when translating human talk.

'If you think you're leaving that thing with me, you've got another think coming!'

'Ah, look at his cute little face. Sure he'd be no trouble at all.'

'Not a chance. I'm going home to pack.'

Una grinned at Finn as the front door slammed shut.

*

The following morning was bright and sunny. When the black Mercedes pulled up outside Una's house, she was already waiting at the gate. The dog was in her arms and a small suitcase stood on the ground beside them. Terrence popped the boot and jumped out to help her with the case but Una was one step ahead of him. She tossed it into the open boot.

He checked his watch. 'Where's Joan?'

Una motioned towards her friend's house. The front door was open and Joan was struggling to manoeuvre a large suitcase through it sideways. Terrence sprinted across the road to help but Joan waved him away.

'I can manage, thank you. You can get the other one though if you don't mind, it's in the hall.'

'Mrs. Cahill, we're only going for a few days, a week at the most. Is all this luggage really necessary?'

'Of course, young man. I was brought up to be prepared for every contingency.'

'Nuclear war included by the looks of it!'

'Oh, thank you for reminding me. Would you be a dear and get my gas mask? I left it in the breakfast room.' He looked at her incredulously. 'I'm only pulling your leg,' she grinned, 'now would you mind carrying my other suitcase to the car?'

He retrieved the second bag from the hall; it was just as big as the first. Una stood waiting by the car, Finn still in her arms. Terrence patted the dog's head.

'Excited to be going on holiday, fella? Plenty of rabbits on the estate for you to chase.'

He made sure the two ladies were settled comfortably in the leather-upholstered back seat before sliding behind the steering wheel. Finn squirmed on Una's lap. She tried to grab his collar but he was too quick for her. Before she could stop him, he'd jumped into the front passenger seat.

'Do you mind? He likes to see where he's going.'

'Not at all. He can drive if he wants.'

'You should probably know, he has a tendency towards motion sickness.'

Just as Terrence started the ignition, Finn made an ominous burping noise.

'Great,' muttered the priest under his breath.

*

They'd only been driving for twenty minutes when they reached their destination. The car slowed down and ground to a halt outside two impressive wrought iron gates. Terrence pulled on the hand brake and got out. He unlatched the gates and had to push hard to get them to swing open. Just inside stood an old disused building. Una assumed it must have been a gate lodge at one time, even though it was twice the size of her own house.

The black Mercedes travelled slowly up a tree-lined avenue, its tyres crunching and grinding on the gravel beneath. The gnarled branches of ancient beech trees entwined overhead creating a tunnel that almost blocked out the sun.

'Old money,' muttered Joan.

'Not at all, Mrs. Cahill. Geraldine's father-in-law was a fisherman, at least that's how he started out. Éamon captained one of a fleet of fishing boats owned by my grandfather. They worked out of Kinsale harbour. He was one of my grandfather's most trusted crew members. They were great friends too, that is until Éamon betrayed him.'

'What happened?' asked Una.

'When the War of Independence broke out, Éamon took things into his own hands. He began using the boat to run guns from Belgium. When he was found out, he hightailed it across the pond to Newfoundland.'

'I take it your grandfather didn't approve of his boat being used for gun-running.'

'He didn't know. It was the British who discovered Éamon's racket but, by that time, he'd gone. He left his wife and son behind, and my grandfather to face the consequences.'

'He must have come back if he bought this place. And he must have done alright for himself in Newfoundland to afford it.'

'He did that alright. When he arrived there, America was in the throes of its Prohibition era. Éamon soon discovered exporting Canadian whisky to the States was far more lucrative than catching cod, not to mention a lot less effort. He got to know old Joe Kennedy and...'

'You don't mean John F. Kennedy's father?' Joan was just as impressed by celebrity as she was by the upper echelons of society.

'The man himself, Mrs. Cahill. The two of them established a mutually-profitable relationship and Éamon carried on smuggling whisky across the border for seven years without getting caught. The old scoundrel made a substantial fortune and decided to quit while he was ahead. He came home in 1928 and reunited with his family. His wife wanted to stay in Cork but Éamon couldn't face my grandfather so he bought this place and they moved up here to Tipperary.'

'Did your grandfather still bear a grudge about the gun-running?'

'It wasn't just that. While Éamon was away, his son William had been secretly courting my Aunt Geraldine. When he came back and sent for his family, William took Geraldine with him. By the time my grandfather got here, they were already married and Aunt Geraldine had become Mrs. William Hennessy.'

Joan was confused. 'But your aunt and her husband were Lord and Lady Hennessy. How did the son of an illegal whiskey trader come by a title?'

Terrence chuckled again. Una liked the fact that he laughed easily, it was the sign of a good nature.

'It came with the house, Mrs. Cahill. You'd be surprised how many defunct titles there are from the time of English rule. Many of them belong to parcels of land and when you buy the land, you acquire the title. When Éamon bought Moonbeg Manor and its estate, it came with what's called a manorial title... in this case Lord of Moonbeg. Manorial titles can be passed down so when Éamon died, William inherited the title and my aunt became Lady Geraldine. Now not everyone is privy to that information, ladies, it's just one of the many skeletons we keep locked away in our family closet.'

'Don't worry,' Una assured him, 'your secret's safe with us.'

They'd been driving through the tree tunnel for a quarter of a mile or so when it ended abruptly and they emerged into bright sunlight. A vast expanse of manicured lawn stretched out before them and an ornate marble fountain stood guard in front of a large country house. It was a magnificent building, Georgian in style and white, like a huge iceberg floating in a sea of green.

A man was driving a ride-on mower back and forth across the grass. When they drew up outside the house, he climbed off it and began making his way towards the car. He arrived just as Terrence got out. Una thought the priest was tall but this man seemed to dwarf him. The big fellow picked him up and hugged him, rocking him back and forth. The dog jumped out of the car and danced around them, barking excitedly.

'Who's this little fella!' The big man's voice was an octave higher than Una had expected from someone with such a massive frame. He bent over and tousled the terrier's head. 'Is he yours, Terry?'

'No, Finn belongs to my aunt. I don't think you ever met Aunt Una, did you Matty? She's my mother's sister.'

Matty hesitated for a moment. 'Is she here?'

'Allow me to introduce you.' Terrence opened the car door. It was Joan who got out first. 'This is Mrs. Cahill, my aunt's companion.' Joan extended her petite hand and the big fellow engulfed it in his.

'Pleased to meet you, missus.'

'And this is Aunt Una,' said Terrence nervously as Una emerged from the car. Matty's pale blue eyes narrowed as he looked her up and down.

'You're a bit short,' he said. Una had always been self-conscious about her diminutive size and found his comment rude, but she decided to let it go.

'I was on the back row when God was giving out the tall genes.'

'Fat too.'

'Now wait a minute, boyo! That's just pig-ignorant!'

'I might be ignorant, missus, but I ain't stupid.' He glared at the priest. 'What's goin' on, Terry? I met your Mam's sister at a funeral years ago, her name's Brigid. Why are ya passing off this woman as your auntie?'

Terrence looked resignedly at Una. 'I told you people underestimate him, didn't I? It seems I'm even guilty of it myself.'

'I thought we were friends,' said the big man, his expression injured.

'I'm sorry, Matty, you're right. Una isn't my aunt at all. Her name's Mrs. Murphy and Joan is her friend, not her companion.'

'Why did ya lie?'

'Listen, Matt, I believe something bad has happened here in this house. I've asked Mrs.

Murphy and her friend to help me find out what it is. I'm sorry I lied to you.'

'Don't you think I want to know the truth just as much as you?'

Una stepped in. 'It's my fault,' she said, talking the blame. 'Terrence did tell us you could be trusted. It was my idea to pose as his aunt, I'm sorry.'

'That's alright, missus, I suppose you don't know me after all. If you did, you'd know Lady Geraldine was more like a mother to me than a boss. I'm terrible shook about what's happened. This last week has been one of the worst of me life.'

Una held out her hand to the big man. 'Will you help us so, Matty?' He took it and surprised her by kissing it.

'I'll do whatever it takes, missus.'

CHAPTER 4

'G'wan in, Terry. I'll put the mower away while you show your friends around. Don't worry about the bags, I'll bring 'em in.'

The priest escorted the two women to an impressive front door. Una thought it must be ten feet high at least. It was painted vermillion red and adorned with polished brass hardware. Terrence lifted the huge Claddagh knocker. He let it fall and they listened as the sound echoed throughout the interior. He was just about to knock again when the heavy door swung open. A short woman stood drying her hands on a small towel. She was about the same height as Una but younger; Una thought mid-thirties. When she saw Terrence, she looked relieved.

'Oh Monsignor! I'm so glad you're here. It's been awful since.....' She dropped the towel and Terrence picked it up. He handed it back to her and she burst into tears. He put his arms around her.

'It's alright, Frances, don't cry. I'm here now.'

She gathered her emotions and glanced down at herself. 'Look at the cut of me,' she said, dabbing her eyes with the towel and sniffing. A white apron covered her simple print dress and her feet were bare. 'I meant to change but... You're early.'

He grabbed her shoulders and held her at arm's length. 'You're a sight for sore eyes, Frances.' He looked down at her bare feet. 'Still having problems?'

'It's me bloody bunions!' she blurted, then clapped her hand over her mouth. 'Beg yer pardon, Father, I didn't mean to swear.'

He flashed her a smile and she blushed. 'Don't worry,' he said. 'I'm sure the Lord knows how much you suffer with those bunions.' She turned her attention to his companions.

'I see you've brought company.'

'Indeed I have.' Terrence looked at the two women and hesitated. He considered continuing the ruse but decided there were far too many holes in it. 'This is Mrs. Murphy and her friend Mrs. Cahill. Una and Joan are old friends of mine.' It wasn't really a lie. They were old, and he did consider them as friends. Frances bobbed a curtsey in the direction of each.

'If you'd like to take the ladies into the drawing room, Father, I'll go and get ye something to eat and drink.'

The priest led the way into a cavernous reception hall. It rose up three storeys, all the way to the roof of the building, and sunlight streamed in through three Venetian windows above the entrance. A wide marble staircase swept up from the centre of the hall to a landing, then twin stairs forked off right and left. Galleries looked down over the hall from the top floor.

The parquet wood flooring was polished to within an inch of its life, as was a large circular table at the centre of the room. The table stood on a hand-woven rug which Joan immediately identified as Aubusson. On it, a display of flowers had been expertly arranged in a tall blue and white vase.

Several heavily-varnished double doors led off the hall. Terrence headed for the nearest and, to Una's surprise, instead of opening inwards, the doors slid apart and disappeared inside the walls. As a spacious reception room was revealed, Una heard Joan's sharp intake of breath. Burgundy silk wall-covering adorned the walls. Its golden highlights shimmered with an almost metallic iridescence as rays of sun slanted in through tall sash windows. A carved marble fireplace provided the focal point of the room, an elaborate Rococo-style affair, and above it was an impressive oil painting of the Rock of Cashel. Elegant mouldings framed the lofty ceiling and a four-tiered crystal chandelier hung from an ornate plaster rose at the centre. Una felt a sense of solemnity, as if she was in a cathedral or a museum.

Joan approached one of two matching antique settees that flanked the marble fireplace. She stroked the Damask silk upholstery.

'Are they real?' she whispered reverently.

'The Chippendales? Ah they're real alright. My aunt and her husband bought most of their furniture from English mansions. Many were demolished back in the 60s and their contents auctioned off. William had a passion for beautiful things; my aunt had an eye for a bargain.'

Joan's attention was drawn to a portrait on the wall. A portly, dark-haired gentleman with a stern expression and a ludicrously full moustache glowered down at them.

'Who's that?' she asked. 'Is he an ancestor?'

The priest laughed. 'I suppose he must be someone's ancestor but he's not ours. I used to call him The Walrus when I was a lad. The Walrus is just another of their acquisitions. William didn't have breeding like Aunt Geraldine. I always got the impression he was trying to buy class. Perhaps he thought if he surrounded himself with the trappings, it would rub off.'

In all the excitement, Una had forgotten about the dog. She suddenly realised he wasn't in the room.

'Where's Finn?' she shrieked. 'Jesus, we have to find him before he breaks something valuable!'

'When did you see him last?' exclaimed Joan.

'When we were out by the car, I think!'

'I'll look outside,' said Terrence, 'you two search the house.'

The two women fanned out through the house shouting Finn's name. Joan was horrified at the prospect of a scruffy terrier wreaking havoc on the exquisite furnishings. Una, despite her insistence that she merely tolerated the animal, was like a mother searching for her lost child.

Terrence found Finn's lead on the ground beside the car. He picked it up and inspected it. The clip wasn't broken. The dog couldn't have freed himself, so that left just one possibility. He called out, not for Finn but for Matty. The big fellow heard his name and poked his head out of a barn door some distance away.

'Looking fer me?' he shouted.

'The dog!' yelled Terrence, running towards the barn.

'A good stretch!' yelled back Matty. 'That's all!' The priest was accustomed to the manner in which his friend's mind worked. He would begin sentences in his head, only uttering them out loud halfway through, as if the listener should somehow know what had gone before.

'Finn,' panted Terrence when he arrived. 'I'm looking for Mrs. Murphy's dog, Finn. Have you seen him?'

'He just needed a good auld run around. The poor craythur wasn't meant to sit on some old lady's lap all day. His little legs needed a good stretch. Sorry, are we in trouble?'

'No, you're not in trouble. As long as he's safe.' Terrence noticed what looked like a camera above the barn door.

'That's new,' he said. 'Who put that up?'

'Ah, the missus had a security company put up a couple of them. We had a break-in a few weeks back.'

'Really?' Terrence had begun to walk back in the direction of the house and Matty lumbered along beside him. The dog ran around them in circles. 'What was stolen?'

'Well, nutt'n, that's what's odd. We've some expensive stuff in there, you know yourself, tools and horse tack and the like, but we couldn't find a single thing missing. The only reason I know we had a break-in is 'cos whoever did it picked the lock. I found the door wide open next morning and the padlock thrown in the grass.

'Were the Guards called?'

'We called 'em alright. They wouldn't come 'cos nutt'n was stolen. I had to go down the station and file a report. Waste o' time.'

'Do you remember what date the break-in was?'

'It was a Tuesday.'

'No, what date was it?'

'Ah, let me think. June fourteenth, that's it. I remember writin' it on the form.'

The front door of the house was ajar and Terrence went straight inside. Matty stopped to take off his wellington boots. He put them on the step and Finn grabbed one. He tried to make off with it but the boot was too heavy. Matty immediately forgot he was in mid-conversation and made a grab for it.

'Ah, so it's a bit o' fun you're after, is it?'

They began a playful tug of war. Whenever Matty managed to wrestle the boot away from him, he'd throw it a few yards and follow as the dog ran to retrieve it, only to start the game over again. It was a good twenty minutes later when Terrence yelled from the door.

'Want something to eat, Matty?' It was the one thing he knew would get his friend's attention.

The big fellow straightened up and grinned. 'Ah g'wan,'

'Come on so, food's on the table. We're in the kitchen.'

Matty made his way through the house, his new best friend close at heel. He found Una, Joan and Terrence seated at a long, refectory-style table which had been scrubbed so often that the wood was pale and worn. Frances was bustling around it. She had wanted to serve tea in the drawing room but Terrence insisted they have it in the kitchen. Joan was disappointed at his choice of venue.

Frances motioned for Matty to sit and pointed to a large plate piled high with ham sandwiches.

'Anybody want one?' he asked. They'd already eaten but he didn't wait for an answer anyway. He pulled the plate towards him and tucked in. The sandwiches disappeared swiftly as he seemed to almost inhale them, one by one. When he'd finished, he wet his finger and ran it around the plate, gathering up the crumbs. He sucked his finger then, satiated, sat back and slapped his hands against his ample belly.

'That steadied the ship up!' he declared.

Joan had been watching with disdain. Terrence was accustomed to his friend's table manners, or lack thereof. He winked at her.

'Got any room left for cake, Matt?' The big man belched without opening his mouth and his blue eyes sparkled.

'Ah g'wan,' he grinned.

He was still holding onto the sandwich plate and Frances suspected he was about to lick it, so she removed it from his big rough hands. She took it away and returned, carrying three dessert plates and some silverware. Then she deposited a large home-made apple crumble cake on the table and cut three modest slices. She put one on each plate and handed them to Una, Joan and Terrence.

'I thought Matty was having cake,' said Joan, confused.

Frances glanced vacantly at the Englishwoman before pushing the remainder of the cake towards the giant-sized man. Finn had been sitting at his feet the whole time and Matty had been surreptitiously passing the odd morsel to him. As soon as he'd polished off the cake, he began to tease the dog. Finn barked his excitement.

'Don't wind him up,' scolded Terrence.

'He's already wound up. I'm unwinding him.'

Una decided it was time they got down to business. 'Tell me, Matty,' she said, 'what do you know about Terrence's two cousins?' By now the big fellow was down on the limestone floor tiles, wrestling with the dog.

'T'ree,' he laughed.

'Tree?' She looked at Terrence but he just shook his head. 'What's a tree got to do with anything?'

'No, *t'ree*. You mean Terry's *t'ree* cousins.'

Again Una looked to Terrence for clarification but he seemed just as bewildered.

'I don't have three cousins,' he said. 'I've just the two.'

'There's Johann and Greta...'

'I know and that's...'

'And then there's Geoff. Hahaa, ya little divil, get outta me pocket! Give me back me hanky.'

'Stop playing with the damn dog!' Terrence was becoming uncharacteristically irritated by his friend's lack of focus. 'Who in God's name is Geoff?'

Matty always knew when he'd pushed Terrence too far. He pulled himself up laboriously from the floor and plopped back onto his seat.

'Greta had a baby when she was fourteen,' he told an open-mouthed Terrence. 'A boy. The family moved from Capetown to Durban and her Mam raised the child as her own.'

The priest was flabbergasted. 'Are you sure? I never.... I had no idea!'

'It's another one of the many skeletons in that family closet of yours, Terry, I only know 'cos the missus told me.'

'Was Greta agreeable to her mother raising the boy?' asked Una.

'Ah poor Greta was never right in the head, even before the baby. Sure that's why they took him off her. She was a darlin' girl mind, clever too like her brother, but she wasn't all there if you know what I mean. After they took the baby, she went off the rails... started drinkin' and takin' drugs.' He shook his head slowly. 'She came to Moonbeg you know.'

'I know,' said Terrence, 'I met her and Johann here once.'

'No. She came about five years ago, on her own. She was here a few days. The missus was delighted when she arrived. She was hoping to get to know her better but it turns out Greta had only come to cadge money off her for drugs. Ah the state of the poor craythur, she was terrible shook. She'd sleep all day and pace the floors at night. They had a fierce row before she left. Lady Geraldine wanted to send her to one of them rehabilitation places but Greta wasn't having it, said she just needed money. The missus tried to stop her leaving, even took her passport off her, but she went anyway.'

'Were they on good terms when she went?' asked Una.

'No, and after she'd gone the missus found out she'd stolen some of her jewellery. Broke the poor auld lady's heart it did.'

'So Greta left without her passport?' asked Una.

'She left without her Irish one anyway,' replied Matty. 'I suppose she must have had a South African one too.'

'I suppose she must,' mused Una. 'Tell me about Johann, Matty. What do you know about him?'

'I know he's not in South Africa any more. He's involved in research somewhere else, where was it now...? Amsterdam! That's it, Amsterdam.'

'Do you know what kind of research?'

'It's funny. I suppose he wanted to help his sister, like fighting poison with poison.'

Once again Matty was conducting a one-sided conversation in his head, leaving his listeners clueless as to its origins or its direction.

'What's funny?' asked Terrence. 'You're not making any sense, Matty. Explain yourself.'

'Johann's research, it's to help drug addicts like Greta. Taking drugs is like taking poison and he studies all kinds of poisons, even the sort spiders and scorpions give when they bite. Fighting poison with poison, see? Doesn't that strike you as funny?'

Una stared into the distance. 'It's ironic, certainly.'

CHAPTER 5

Matty was back on the floor with the dog. Finn was rooting in the big man's trouser pocket for a handkerchief he'd found there earlier. Between Matty's raucous laughter and the dog's playful growls, they were creating an almighty commotion that reverberated around the cavernous kitchen. Joan leaned in to Una.

'What do you think about this Johann fellow, dear? Is he a suspect?'

'A prime one I'd say. He has access to toxins.'

Joan tried to point out once again that the toxicology report had come back negative, but she couldn't make herself heard above the din.

'Why don't you take him out for a *walk*?' yelled Una. Finn recognised the word and stopped what he was doing immediately.

He spat out the handkerchief, which was now in tatters anyway, and looked from Una to Matty and back. The big fellow needed no further encouragement, he motioned for the little terrier to follow him and together they left the kitchen.

'Thank the Lord for that,' said Una, when they'd gone. 'I couldn't hear myself think.'

'That's typical of Matty,' laughed Terrence, 'maddening and endearing at the same time.'

'Endearing?' exclaimed Joan. 'Well that word didn't immediately spring to mind. His table manners are far from endearing. The man is like a thirteen year-old boy in a giant's body.'

'All part of his charm, Mrs. Cahill,' replied the priest, still laughing.

Una put both hands palm down on the table in a business-like gesture, as if drawing a line under Matty's shenanigans.

'Right,' she said, 'now that we have some peace and quiet we can recap. Have you discovered anything new, Terrence?'

'Only that the barn was broken into a few weeks ago.'

'Oh?'

'Nothing was taken apparently, but Aunt Geraldine had security cameras installed anyway.'

'That's good. Surveillance camera footage can be very useful. One of the real life crime programmes I watch on telly is dedicated solely to crimes solved using security cameras. We'll have a look at the tapes, you never know.'

'I expect they'll be in my aunt's office.'

'Alright, now let's think. If those two unfortunate women were murdered, we have to decide on the most likely motive.'

'Money.' Joan had been quiet up to this point. 'Financial gain. What about Greta? She came to borrow money from her aunt.'

Una nodded. 'We can't rule her out. If she still has a drug habit, she'll need money to fund it. But would she have the clarity of thought to plan a murder, or the means to carry it out? My money's on Johann, I think he's the most likely person of interest here.'

Frances had been washing the dishes at the far end of room and now she came over with a fresh pot of tea.

'Sit down and have a cup with us,' said Una, motioning towards a chair. Her tone was that of a school mistress so Frances sat down. It was Joan who addressed her.

'Who found Lady Geraldine's body, my dear?'

'I did, missus. She used to come down for her breakfast at seven on the dot. Same time, same breakfast every morning - one softly-boiled egg and a piece of dry toast cut into soldiers. When she wasn't down by eight, I went up to check on her. The bedroom door was open and I found the poor craythur lying on her bed.' The cook's voice began to crack and she pulled out a small white handkerchief from her apron pocket. 'Face down, she was.' She dabbed at a tear that rolled down her cheek.

'You mentioned her bedroom door being open,' said Una. 'Was that unusual?'

'It was. The missus always slept with the door shut, she didn't like draughts.'

'And where was the housekeeper all this time?'

'In her room. I ran straight there to tell her. She didn't seem as upset as I thought she'd be, but then Lelia's always been the practical one. We went back together and Lelia checked the missus for a pulse, said she was cold. She went straight downstairs and phoned for an ambulance. When they came, they said she'd been dead for hours.' Frances dabbed at her eyes again. 'It was her birthday only the day before,' she sniffed. 'We had a little do for her, just the missus and us staff, it was grand. None of us knew it'd be the last time we'd ever see her alive...' She began to sob now and Joan patted her arm.

'There there, my dear.'

'I didn't know it was her birthday,' said Terrence, 'I'd have sent her something, or at least telephoned.' It occurred to Una that at last she might have a trail to follow.

'Did she receive any gifts for her birthday?' she asked. The cook dried her eyes.

'We gave her presents. Nothing much, just tokens. Matty made her a tiny wooden rocking horse, beautiful little thing, and Lelia gave her a pair of soft leather gloves. I knitted her a lilac scarf. Lilac's her favourite colour. I mean it *was* her favourite colour.'

'Do you think we could take a look at her room, Frances?' asked Una.

'You can o'course, I'll take ye.'

The three of them followed the cook out of the kitchen and into the entrance hall. A short walk past the circular table took them to the base of the vast staircase. Una and Joan looked up in unison to see a gigantic chandelier hanging from the roof. It shimmered as the light from the Venetian windows bounced off its pendent crystals, like sunshine on raindrops.

'Jayzus,' gasped Una, 'now I know how the Pope feels.'

Terrence grinned. 'Not bad for an Irish bootlegger, is it?'

He and Frances started up the stairs and the two friends followed. They went to opposing sides of the staircase and grabbed a broad handrail each to aid their ascent. At the top of the first flight of steps was a spacious landing with staircases leading off left and right. Una wasn't sure how many more steps she could climb so was relieved when Frances led them to a door on that floor. It turned out to be not just a bedroom but a suite of rooms. The first was a sitting room. Three of its walls were wood-panelled. The other was lined from floor to ceiling with shelves that groaned under the weight of books, some of them huge. Terrence said his aunt liked to collect antique books and, indeed, books about antiques.

'She liked to keep abreast of the market,' he told them. 'She kept her eye on the value of what she had and the prices of the things she wanted to buy. She drove a hard bargain and she never paid a penny more than something was worth.'

'Your aunt certainly had impeccable taste,' commented Joan. 'The house is exquisitely furnished and decorated.'

'But what good did it do her?' replied Una. 'It's just stuff at the end of the day. Now she's gone and it's all still here.'

'I don't agree.' Joan was adamant. 'Lady Geraldine surrounded herself with beautiful things which made her happy while she was alive. What's wrong with that?'

Terrence joined in the debate. 'I have to side with Una on this one,' he said. 'It's all just stuff. That's why I think the whole thing should be turned over to An Taisce.'

'The best idea altogether,' agreed Una. 'That way people can come and enjoy your aunt's house and her things, and the money they pay goes towards helping the local economy.'

By this time, they were through into Geraldine's bed chamber. At the request of the Gardaí it hadn't been cleaned or tidied since she'd been found, but there didn't seem to be much out of place. The bedspread still bore the impression of a body but there were no signs of violence or a struggle.

After a cursory look around, Una asked Frances to take them to the housekeeper's room. They retraced their steps back out onto the landing, past both sets of stairs and over to the far side of the house. There were four rooms on this side and they all had smaller doors. Frances opened one and they stepped inside.

Lelia's room was modest. A pair of matching night tables flanked a double bed with its brass bedstead. A washstand stood opposite and, apart from a simple chair, the only other piece of furniture in the room was an oak wardrobe. The bed remained unmade. Una addressed Frances.

'So you found Lelia's body as well as Lady Geraldine's?'

Frances sensed that something was being implied and it unsettled her.

'Well, yes... but I wasn't on my own. When Lelia didn't show up for breakfast the day after I found the missus dead, there was no way I was going to her room on my own. I went and fetched Matty. We came up together.'

'And where exactly did ye find her?'

'In bed. Her dressing gown was on the floor and her slippers were at the side of the bed.'

'Where are they now?'

'I put them in the wardrobe out of the way. The paramedics were trampling all over them, it didn't seem right.'

'Can we see?'

Frances pulled open the door of the wardrobe and Una looked inside. Various items of clothing hung neatly on a rail and a row of shoes was arranged in pairs below them. As Frances said, a gown had been thrown in, the understandable act of a distraught cook. Una drew aside a couple of dresses.

'What's that?'

A handkerchief had been stuffed inside one of the shoes. She pulled it out and some items of jewellery fell onto the floor. Frances peered at them.

'Those belong to Lady Geraldine. What on earth are they doing in Lelia's wardrobe?'

'Unless I'm very much mistaken,' replied Una, 'you weren't the first to find your employer. If you ask me, Lelia found her before you she and used the opportunity to help herself.'

Terrence thought Una's conclusion was hasty at best. 'But Lelia was with my aunt for years,' he said. 'I don't for a minute believe she'd steal from her.'

'Don't forget she was about to lose her job,' Una reminded him. 'If there's no Lady Geraldine, there's no job. Perhaps she thought she was entitled to a little severance bonus after all her years of service.'

The priest bent down and picked up a brooch shaped like a bee. It was crafted from yellow gold and black diamonds.

'This is my aunt's alright. I remember her wearing it on special occasions.'

'Careful,' warned Una. 'It could have traces of poison on it.' Terrence dropped the brooch as if it was a red hot coal.

'Don't be ridiculous,' he said, wiping his hand on his trouser leg. 'We should inform the Guards about this.'

'Not yet. If there's one thing the police don't like doing, it's reopening closed cases. We'll need more concrete evidence before we can convince them to do that.'

CHAPTER 6

An eerie silence descended on the room as those gathered stared down at the incongruous items of jewellery on the floor. It was Una who broke the spell.

'Come on,' she said, 'let's all go back downstairs. We're finding more questions than answers up here. A nice cuppa should help clarify our thought processes.'

They retraced their steps down the marble staircase and, on their arrival in the kitchen, Frances busied herself making tea. The others resumed their places at the table. Joan was the first to volunteer her theory.

'If anyone murdered anyone, I think the housekeeper killed her mistress,' she declared. 'I think her own death was one of misadventure.' Terrence, having already made his mind up that foul play was involved, was more than eager to hear a congruent opinion.

'So you think Lelia murdered my aunt?'

Joan nodded. 'And I think the jewellery we found in her room had something to do with it.'

'It's a possibility,' said Una, 'but I'm not convinced Lelia would be capable, not if she worked alone.'

'So you think it's a conspiracy?' Terrence was like a drowning man grabbing for any floating object. Una shook her head.

'Conspiracy theories are just a lazy person's way of dismissing something obvious that's been overlooked. Besides, I left my tin foil hat in Ballyanny.'

Frances brought over a tray. On it was a large pot of tea along with four china cups and saucers.

'Ah good,' said Una, 'I'm glad you brought a cup for yourself, Frances, sit down. There are a few things I need to have clear in my mind.'

'Whatever I can do to help,' the cook replied meekly. She poured the tea and sat down.

'Now then, the jewellery we found in Lelia's wardrobe. Did you ever see your mistress wearing it?'

'Like the Monsignor said, she wore that sort of thing on special occasions. The only pieces she wore on a regular basis were her wedding ring and a string of pearls, and she wore them every day.'

'I noticed the string of pearls on her night table,' said Joan. 'Beautiful ten millimeter gems, opera length.'

'You would notice that. Well I'm not going to venture an opinion yet as to the murderer's identity, but I do believe the housekeeper was the first to find Lady Geraldine, and that she stole those jewels. I also think it was just a crime of opportunity, but one that backfired on her.'

'No conspiracy then?' Terrence seemed disappointed.

'I didn't say that. I don't know anything for certain yet. What I do know is your friend has been gone with my dog for far too long. Where on earth could they have got to?'

'God only knows,' grinned Terrence, 'the woods maybe. Matty has a new playmate so he won't be back 'til he's hungry, although that shouldn't be long.'

Frances looked at her watch. 'Jayzus,' she shrieked. 'Look at the time!' She glanced at Terrence and blushed. 'Sorry for swearing, Father, I'm late getting dinner started.'

'You're forgiven, Frances. We'll get out from under your feet.'

'Before we go,' said Una, 'do you know where the surveillance tapes are kept?'

'They're DVDs, missus, and they're in the study. Will I show you where it is?'

Terrence waved her away. 'No need, I know the way. Is the computer password still the same, Frances?'

'Yes... one two three four five.'

'A hacker's dream,' mumbled Una.

'Aunt Geraldine had no time for technology,' explained Terrence. 'She refused to get a computer until she found out she could buy antiques online. Now if you'd like come with me, ladies.'

Una and Joan followed him down a narrow hallway, the walls of which were lined with dark oak panelling. They passed several doors before they reached the end, only to come face-to-face with a solid panelled wall.

Una frowned at Terrence. 'Perhaps we should have asked Frances to show us the way after all.'

'Ah, ye of little faith,' he grinned, pushing against one of the panels. They heard the faint click of a lock and the panel swung inward.

'A secret door!' gasped Joan. 'How exciting!'

He led them into a dark and windowless room. When he flipped a light switch just inside the door, four wall scones jumped into life illuminating the room with soft, subdued light. A mahogany desk stood at the centre and on top was a telephone, monitor and keyboard. Terrence was delighted with himself.

'It's a priest hole,' he announced. 'We're in the oldest part of the house. They used to hide Catholic priests here during Penal Times.'

'I know what a priest hole is,' barked Una. 'I've just never been inside one.'

Joan was thrilled to find herself in a hidden room.

'Are there any secret passages?' she gushed. 'Miss Marple was always discovering some secret passage or other in old manor houses like this.'

'No secret passages I'm afraid, just the room.'

'Oh but it's wonderful,' she sighed. Even Una had to admit it was ingenious. After a brief scan of the room she pulled a buttoned leather captain's chair out from the desk.

'Sit down, Terrence,' she said, 'and fire up that computer. We have work to do.'

Two straight-backed chairs stood against the wall and Una pulled one over to sit beside him, motioning for Joan to do the same with the other. It wasn't long before he had the computer up and running. In one of the desk drawers they found a box containing the security discs and one by one they fast-forwarded through them. After two long hours, the most interesting thing they'd come across was a curious badger.

'Well that was a waste of time.' Terrence yawned and stretched up his arms, linking his fingers above his head.

'Check her search history,' instructed Una. 'Perhaps that'll turn up something.' Geraldine's search history proved equally unrewarding. 'There's nothing else for it, we'll have to look through her emails.'

'She wouldn't like us going through her personal correspondence,' protested the priest.

'She's hardly in a position to object, is she, and our intentions are honourable.'

'I suppose so.' Terrence opened up his aunt's email account. 'Holy Mother of God, look at this lot!'

'It's good that she hasn't deleted them. Now don't bother opening anything that doesn't look personal, otherwise we'll still be here this time next week.'

Terrence scrolled down through the pages of Geraldine's inbox as the two women watched. Most were junk mails promoting everything from magazine subscriptions to online dating and dodgy investment opportunities.

They didn't see anything of a personal nature until they were half a dozen or so pages in, then Terrence spotted an email from Greta dated four months earlier. Her surname was Burton now and it appeared that she'd finally accepted Geraldine's offer. At her aunt's expense, she had undergone a rehabilitation programme at a specialist institution; she was writing to express her gratitude at finally being drug and alcohol free.

'Oh well,' sighed Joan, 'I suppose that means we can rule out Greta. That suspect list of yours is getting shorter by the day, dear.'

'I'm not taking her off the list, I'm just moving her down it. Terrence, is there nothing at all you can tell us about Geoff?'

'How could I? I only found out he existed the same time you did. If Greta had him when she was fourteen, then that would make him twenty now, give or take a year.'

'Did you know,' offered Joan, 'that a young person's frontal cortex isn't fully developed until they're in their twenties? I read an article about it the other day.'

Terrence looked askance at the Englishwoman, as if she was mad. Una, on the other hand, was perfectly in tune with her friend's train of thought.

'You're on the right path there, Joanie, but it's the prefrontal cortex. It was on an episode of Forensic Files only last week.'

'What on earth are you two women talking about?'

'Oh, Forensic Files is one of Una's favourite TV programmes!' Joan told him. 'They show how forensic science is used to solve violent crimes and mysterious accidents. It's frightfully good.'

'No, I mean this frontal cortex thing. What's it got to do with Geoff?'

'Not frontal,' Una corrected, 'it's prefrontal. It means that young people don't have the inhibitory responses found in a fully-formed adult's brain. It means they can be subject to rage, bouts of extreme anger.'

'I see. Do you think this could be a rage killing?'

'I don't,' said Joan. 'A rage killing is unplanned. Something so spontaneous would leave a trail, obvious clues. In my opinion, whatever this is has been well thought out.'

'You're right, pet,' agreed Una. 'It does appear to be the premeditated work of a mature mind.'

'How do we find out who's responsible?' asked Terrence.

A sly smile crept across Una's face. 'We wait.'

'For what?'

'An attempt on your life.'

'I sincerely hope you have a plan B, Mrs. Murphy. Plan A doesn't appeal to me at all.'

'Plan B is we find out what killed your aunt, then we work backwards to find the killer.'

'That's more like it. Don't get me wrong. I'm looking forward to the day I meet my maker. I just hadn't planned on it being quite so soon.'

CHAPTER 7

Frances announced that dinner was about to be served. Much to Joan's delight, they were to eat in the formal dining room and Terrence led the way. Yet another pair of massive double doors opened onto another large, bright room. A highly-polished table ran almost the full length and stood on a silk Persian rug which, although still impressive, was beginning to look a little worn in the more heavily-trafficked areas. Carver chairs with plush red upholstery were positioned at either end of the table, and matching chairs stood in neat rows on either side. A chandelier hung down over the centre of the table and two silver candelabras flanked it. More portraits of other people's ancestors adorned the walls in gilt frames, and glass cabinets displayed collections of crystal and china. Five places had been set at one end of the table and a variety of lidded serving dishes promised a plentiful meal. It was the first time Terrence had dined at the table without his aunt being present. He hesitated for a moment, then seated the two women on either side of the top seat before taking his place at the head of the table.

They'd just made themselves comfortable when Matty returned with Finn. The dog's jaws were locked onto the big man's jeans so he was having to drag one leg behind him. Frances followed him in carrying the final two serving dishes.

'You're just in time,' Una told him.

'I know, missus.' He grinned broadly as he sat down next to her. 'Me nose tells me when food's ready.' This was Matty's favourite time of day, in fact every mealtime was Matty's favourite time of day.

'What's fer dinner Francie?' he asked, rubbing his hands together.

'Does it matter?'

'Not at all. Sure as long as there's enough fer everyone.'

'I should think so, I boiled five pounds of spuds!'

'Well that's me sorted so. What's everyone else having?'

Joan was appalled. It wasn't her idea of polite dinner conversation. Frances noticed her look of distaste.

'Don't mind us, it's just a bit of banter.'

'But surely when your mistress was here...' Joan felt certain their exchanges must have been less familiar when the lady of the house was present.

'The missus?' laughed Frances. 'Sure she enjoyed the craic as much as the next man. Always had the last word too.'

'Sounds like you, dear.' Joan glanced at her friend to gauge her response, but Una wasn't biting.

'She who speaks last, speaks best,' she said airily.

Frances was eating with them so she sat down and began passing around the various serving dishes. Una's mind wasn't on food.

'Tell me, Matty,' she said, 'what do you know about Geoff?'

The big fellow already had half a potato stuffed into his mouth.

'Geofffooo?'

'Lady Geraldine's nephew Geoff.'

Matty gulped down enough food to enable him to speak. 'Oh him. Sure I never met Geoff. He never came here, did he Frances?' Frances shook her head as she offered the gravy boat to Joan.

'He sent a photograph of himself to the missus when he graduated from university a few years back,' she said. 'It's in her bedside drawer I think. He was probably hoping she'd send him money. I expect she did.'

Una was disappointed. 'Don't either of you know anything at all about him?'

'He's a clever lad,' offered Matty, 'takes after his mother. He was only fourteen when he took what we'd call the Leaving Cert. He's studying to be a doctor now.'

'Geoff is training to be a physician?' Una waited while Matty swallowed the contents of his mouth.

'Not that kind of doctor, missus.'

'You mean he's taking a Doctorate?'

Matty had his finger in the air, as if about to speak, but again Una would have to wait for an answer. Having succeeded in consuming half a potato in one go, he was now attempting an entire one and it was proving to be more of a challenge than he'd anticipated.

'Spit it out, man,' barked Terrence, testily.

Matty stopped chomping and, for a moment, they all feared he might do exactly that. Terrence was immediately sorry for shouting.

'Never mind,' he said. 'Eat up, my friend. We'll talk later.'

Matty needed no further encouragement. He finished off his spuds, then proceeded to devour everything else within reach. Finn sat at his feet, hoping for a bite, but Matty was so engrossed with the task at hand that he forgot the dog was there, so no tasty morsels were forthcoming this time.

Joan sat across from him but kept her eyes on her plate. His lack of manners appalled her. Una, on the other hand, was transfixed. She watched in amazement as he gobbled up everything in sight.

'Do you think we should find out what's he's doing?' said Terrence.

'Well he's certainly not masticating!' declared Joan haughtily. Matty stopped eating and shot her a quizzical look.

'No, I meant Geoff. Do you think we should find out what Geoff's doing?'

'Of course,' said Una. 'He certainly can't be overlooked.'

'How would we go about finding him?'

'Social media's the most obvious. He's a millennial. All millennials use Facebook or Twitter, or both. Social media's as important to their generation as a telephone was to ours.'

'What about Johann? How would we locate him?'

'We'll try LinkedIn. That tends to be the network of choice for professionals.'

'And Greta?'

'Greta's easy, we have an email from her. All we have to do is send her a return one, informing her of your aunt's death. In fact we should go back through all Geraldine's emails. Greta was thanking her for stumping up the money for rehab, so there must have been previous correspondence between them. Perhaps your aunt saved her personal mails to a folder.'

'Good thinking. Aunt Geraldine was fairly organised when it came to keeping records, especially where there was money involved.'

'Well from what I hear, those rehabilitation clinics don't come cheap. I'm sure there will have been a substantial debit involved. We'll go back through her records and at the same time we'll eliminate Greta from our suspect list. Given Geraldine's kindness and generosity towards her, she's the least likely to wish her harm.'

After dinner, Terrence escorted the two women back to the priest hole for a more detailed search of his aunt's records. Joan had spotted a filing cabinet and in it she found a box file containing old cheque books. She began searching through the stubs for anything relevant while Terrence logged into his aunt's bank account online. Una divided her attention between the two. It wasn't long before Terrence found what he was looking for.

'Got it!' he declared triumphantly. 'There's a cheque recorded on the fourth of December. It was made payable to a company in Durban. The amount is eight thousand, three hundred and eighty-two euro and six cents.'

'Goodness me!' exclaimed Joan. 'Such a lot of money, and such an odd amount!'

Terrence peered at the screen again. 'There's a note underneath the transaction. It converted to exactly 130,000 South African rand at the time.'

Una slapped him on the back. 'Good man! Joanie, search the cheque stubs. See if you can find it.'

Joan thumbed through the cheque books looking for a matching stub.

'Nothing here for that date.'

'The cheque number ends 2138,' Terrence told her. Joan flipped through the stubs once more.

'It's gone!' she exclaimed. 'That one's been ripped out!'

'Doesn't surprise me,' muttered Terrence. The two women stared at him, waiting for an explanation. 'Well we're back to skeletons in the closet, aren't we. Aunt Geraldine wasn't about to advertise the fact that a member of her family was a drug addict. She guarded her reputation fiercely, I'm not at all surprised she wanted to destroy all evidence of it. I'm sure she would have deleted Greta's emails too, given time.'

Una thought for a moment. 'Alright so,' she said, 'we'll take a more direct approach. Terrence, get back on that computer and search South Africa's telephone listings. We're looking for the surname Burton in the Durban area.'

Terrence lost no time and soon came up with the goods. 'Eleven listings for Burton in the Durban area,' he announced.

'Grand.' Una was surprised there were so few in a city that size. 'What time is it there now?'

Again Terrence rattled away on the computer keys. 'Durban is two hours ahead of us. It's eight o'clock in the evening there.'

Una picked up the telephone handset and held it out to him. 'Start calling.'

He hit the jackpot on his fourth call. The two women could only hear one side of the conversation, but it began the same way as the first three.

'Good evening, my name is Monsignor McCarthy. I'm ringing from Ireland. I'm trying to trace my cousin, Greta Burton, and I wondered if...' There was a pause as whoever was on the other end interrupted him. He frowned at Una and she shrugged her shoulders. 'No, she doesn't owe me money, why would you....?' There was another pause, this time much longer, and Una watched as his complexion turned ashen.

'I see,' he said finally. 'Well I'm very sorry to hear that. Please accept my sincere condolences and I apologise for troubling you at this difficult time. Yes, of course I will remember her at Mass. Yes, thank you. Goodbye.' He replaced the handset slowly and Una put her hand on his arm.

'Does that mean what I think it means?'

He nodded. 'Greta died last week. They think it was an accidental drug overdose. Johann is already there for the funeral; he took a flight out of Amsterdam yesterday.' The priest slumped back in his chair. 'I'm sorry, ladies, would you excuse me? I'd like a few moments alone.'

'Of course, of course.' Una was already ushering Joan out of the room. 'Take as long as you need, we'll get Frances to put the kettle on. We'll be in the drawing room when you're ready.'

The two women made their way back to the entrance hall and, from there, Una branched off to the kitchen. Joan headed for the drawing room and her friend joined her there a few minutes later. A fire had been lit and they sat either side of it, glad of its warmth. Even though it was a warm evening, the cavernous room felt cold. They sat in silence, staring into the flames, until finally Joan spoke.

'Three women. Two from the same family and a member of staff die within a week of each other on two different continents. I have to admit, Una, I still thought Geraldine and Lelia's deaths might be a coincidence. Now I'm not so sure.'

'Don't tell me you still have a shred of doubt!'

'Drug addicts do have a high rate of recidivism, dear.'

Una laughed. 'Who are you trying to convince, Joanie? Me or you?'

'Myself probably.' Joan sighed. 'Where has Frances got to with that tea? If ever I needed the cup that cheers but not inebriates, it's now.'

Una sighed too. 'I'd happily settle for one that inebriates.'

Murder at the Big House

CHAPTER 8

Frances had just brought in the tea things when Matty arrived back with Finn. Una was glad of the opportunity to question him without the priest being there. The big fellow plopped his full weight down onto the other end of Joan's sofa, causing the prim Englishwoman to bounce up into the air. She assumed a haughty expression and slid as far away from him as she could. Finn danced around his feet, determined to keep the attention focused on himself.

'We had fun, didn't we boy!' he said, ruffling the little dog's scruffy head. 'He's a grand little fella.'

A three-tiered cake stand stood among the tea things and Matty reached for a French Fancy. He broke off a small corner and gave it to the dog, then popped the remainder of the cake into his mouth. Joan scowled at Una.

'Well he certainly seems to like you,' said Una, ignoring her friend. 'Tell me more about Geoff. What else do you know about him?'

The last time he'd made Una wait for an answer he got into trouble, so he didn't wait to swallow. Instead he tried to speak around the mass of sponge cake, buttercream and fondant icing in his mouth.

'Mot mutt.' Particles of cake sprayed out in all directions. Joan rolled her eyes and retreated further into her corner. Matty swallowed and wiped his mouth on his sleeve. 'Not much. He likes his rugby, I know dat.'

'Do you play yourself? You've the build for a forward.'

He smiled. 'I used to play, missus, when I was younger. Fer a couple o' seasons, I was a reserve player fer the National team. Then me shoulder got banjaxed.'

'Really?' Una was impressed. 'I had no idea. I'm sorry about your shoulder. You say Geoff is keen on the game. Does he play himself or is he just a fan?'

'Ah, he plays alright. He's in the Baby Boks.'

'What's that?'

'South Africa's under-twenties. Geoff's a good player by all accounts; they say he'll go on to join the Springboks. He's a big lad, taller than Terrence but heavier, plays second row.

'Interesting. Would you mind doing me a favour, Matty?

'If I'm able, missus.'

'Would you bring in our bags, please? I think they're still in the boot of Terry's car.'

'I will o'course.' He jumped up immediately. 'I meant to do it before but I got distracted.'

He was out of the room in a couple of bounds, with Finn close behind him. Una watched him leave then sat in silence, staring into the fire and sipping her tea.

'A penny for them,' said Joan, startling her from her reverie.

'What? Ah, they're not even worth that, pet.'

'I know you, Una Murphy. I can almost hear those cogs turning in that brain of yours.'

'That's the problem, Joanie, turning is all they're doing at the moment.' Just then Terrence joined them.

'Here you are,' he said, 'I went looking for you in the kitchen.'

'What is the point of us sitting in the kitchen,' said Joan, 'when we have all these beautiful rooms at our disposal?'

He laughed. 'I suppose you're right. Did I hear Matt's voice?'

'You did,' replied Una. 'I asked him to bring in our bags. I assume we've been allocated accommodation.'

'Frances has made up beds in two adjoining guest rooms. I'm sure you'll be comfortable there.'

'That's very kind. Are you feeling better now, Terrence?'

'Better?'

'Yes, you seemed distressed about Greta's death.'

'Ah it wasn't that exactly, I hardly knew her after all. It's just the sad irony of it. Poor Greta was just getting her life back together and...' He heard a noise and looked up to see Matty in the doorway, juggling two large suitcases and Una's overnight bag.

'Did I hear right, Terry? Is Greta dead?'

'I'm afraid so, my friend.'

'Ah sweet Jayzus, what in the name of all that's holy is goin' on?' The big man turned on his heels and shortly after, they heard him trudging up the staircase with his load. Finn didn't follow this time, instead he sat on the rug and stared fixedly at Una. She put down her cup.

'Come on, Finn,' she said, 'you want your dinner don't you.'

'How do you know what he wants?' asked Terrence. 'Are you a mind reader now?'

'Reading minds becomes second nature when you've spent as many years teaching primary school children as I have.' She hauled herself up off the settee and made her way to the kitchen where she'd left the dog's food and dish. She metered out the usual amount of his favourite meat and Finn wolfed it down greedily. He looked for more.

'Alright.' She spooned another small helping into his bowl. 'But that's your lot.'

'Must be all that exercise,' she told them on her return to the drawing room. 'The poor dog was ravenous.'

'On the subject of food,' said Terrence, 'I'm going into Fethard tomorrow. If you want to join me, we could have lunch there. It's high time I made funeral arrangements so I have to go into McCarthys.'

'Are they relatives of yours?' asked Joan.

'No, these are the Tipperary McCarthys. Why don't you come? They have a superb menu.'

'The undertaker serves food?' Joan was puzzled.

'Well it's not just an undertakers, McCarthys is one of the old-school establishments. It's a bar and restaurant too, there aren't many of them left anymore. It used to be a grocery and hardware shop as well, but that part of it closed.'

'Ah yes,' said Una, 'I remember them well. One stop shopping, cradle to grave. Those places are few and far between now, more's the pity.'

'Indeed. McCarthys is a gem of a place, Matty's well-known in there.'

'What for?' enquired Joan. 'Eating them out of house and home?'

Terrence laughed. 'No doubt he could, but that's not the reason. They tell a story about him. Matt had a hunter gelding once, big old beast it was. They say he tried to ride it into the bar one day, but he couldn't fit it through the door so he tied it up outside and took out a couple of pints, one for himself and one for the horse. The story goes they didn't stop at one and the horse ended up stocious, fell on top of Matty and the two of them slept there 'til morning.'

'I'm not familiar with the expression,' said Joan. 'Does stocious mean tired?'

'It's means drunk, pet,' Una told her.

'Disgraceful!' Joan was appalled. 'Is it true, Terrence?'

'That's how the story goes, Mrs. Cahill. Whether or not it's true I couldn't say. The Irish rarely let facts stand in the way of a good story. Anyway, I thought you ladies might be interested in seeing the old place.'

'Why don't you take Matty instead?' suggested Una. 'Joan and I want to poke around here.'

'Fair enough. Well I'm going to turn in, it's been a long day. I'll bid you ladies goodnight.'

'Perfect,' whispered Una, when he'd gone. 'We have some serious sleuthing to do tomorrow, Joanie, and we need the men out from under our feet.'

'Well hopefully they'll eat at McCarthys too because if I have to watch that big oaf bury his face in another plate of food, I won't be responsible for my actions.'

Una chuckled. 'Try not to dream about it, pet, me and Finn are off to bed.' She started for the door and the dog followed. 'Goodnight, Joanie.'

'Goodnight, my dear. I won't be far behind you. I think I heard Frances go up. I just want to wash up these few things first.'

Una smiled to herself as she mounted the steps. She knew full well Joan wouldn't sleep a wink if she thought the dishes would go unwashed overnight. She was already halfway up when she realised Finn wasn't with her. She looked back to see him sitting at the foot of the stairs.

'What are you waiting for? You don't expect me to carry you, do you?' The little dog stood, wagged his tail and sat down again. 'Alright,' she sighed, 'just this once mind.'

She went back and picked him up. 'This isn't fair,' she said, looking into his liquid brown eyes. 'You've four legs, I've only the two.' Finn gave her face a quick lick and Una tucked him under one arm. She grabbed the banister and together the old woman and her little dog slowly ascended the grand staircase.

CHAPTER 9

When Una and Joan arrived down for breakfast, they found Terrence and Matty already seated at the dining table. They'd all given Frances their preferences the night before and while Joan had ordered a soft boiled egg, Una had opted for toast and marmalade. Terrence had asked for a Full Irish, as had Matty, but when Frances brought in the big man's plate, Joan thought it might be better described as an Epic Irish. She kept her eyes on her own plate so she wouldn't have to watch him eat. Her lips were pressed so tightly together that Una was surprised she managed to squeeze anything at all through them.

During breakfast, the priest announced his plans had changed. Archbishop Laughlin had phoned first thing summoning him to review some legal matters, and he wasn't sure how long he'd be gone. It was possible he might return later that night but he could be gone for a couple of days. Matty said he'd go into Fethard anyway. His Mam lived there and he hadn't seen her for a couple of weeks. The new arrangement was perfectly acceptable to Una as it still left her and Joan to their own devices.

When the men had gone, the friends went for a stroll around the walled garden, allowing Finn his morning constitutional. Once back inside, Joan took herself on a self-guided tour of the house while Una headed for Geraldine's suite of rooms. She wanted to examine the scene of the crime at her leisure, with no one to distract her.

She opened the outer door and stood on the threshold, taking everything in. The furniture was an eclectic mixture of styles, mostly belonging to the eighteenth and nineteenth centuries. A matching pair of French-style chairs stood either side of a deep window and an elegant little writing desk was positioned under a lighted sconce on the wall. On it sat a silver and cut-crystal inkwell set.

The fireplace had a similar surround to the one in the drawing room, only smaller. A pale blue Persian rug covered most of the parquet wood floor, giving the wood-panelled room a less gloomy appearance than it would otherwise have, and a crystal chandelier dangled from the ceiling. The room felt cluttered to Una, especially as one of its walls was lined with books.

Finn stood beside his mistress for a minute or so but then the temptation proved too much. It was a new place to explore after all so he trotted right in, his tail as straight as a flagstaff. The movement broke Una's concentration.

'Finn! Come back here, you little....' Before she could think of a fitting epithet, the terrier gave her a dismissive backward glance, wagged his tail and broke into a run, heading in the direction of Geraldine's bed chamber. Una hurried after him, only too aware of what havoc he was capable of wreaking. When she arrived, she found him sniffing intently at the door of an ornate armoire.

'What have you got there?'

His tail was no longer in the air. He had it tucked between his legs and was snuffling eagerly at the gap where the two doors met. Una opened one of the doors and Finn leapt straight inside. He sniffed his way around the floor of the wardrobe, giving the occasional snort or sneeze, until he eventually fixated on an area by the door.

'Did you find something, Finn?'

She tried to push him out of the way but he pushed back.

'You stubborn little….' Una's one-sided conversations with her dog often ended unfinished in this way.

She finally managed to forcibly remove him and tossed him to one side. The interior of the wardrobe was dark and she couldn't see a thing, but Una knew her dog's nose had detected something of interest so she watched him. He began to track, his tail still tucked tightly underneath him. He inched slowly across the floor, his nose close to the rug, moving his head from side to side as if following a scent. He snorted and sniffed his way from the wardrobe to the bed, where he seemed to lose track of whatever he'd been following, then he did what any self-respecting dog would do. He rolled on the ground to transfer the scent onto himself. Una watched him intently.

'What's going on?'

Una almost jumped out of her skin. 'Joan!' she exclaimed, clutching her chest. 'You scared the bejeezus outta me! How long have you been there?'

'I just arrived. Did you find anything?'

Una jutted her chin in the direction of the dog. 'I wish we could ask him the same question.' Joan's arrival had distracted the terrier from his mission and he'd jumped up onto the bed.

'Get off that beautiful bedlinen, you wretched beast,' shrieked Joan, flapping her arms. Finn interpreted her animated actions as an invitation to play and bounded around the bed, barking with excitement. When she didn't join in, he stopped and stared at her, his eyes bright, his pink tongue lolling from his mouth.

'If I didn't know better, Una, I'd swear that dog of yours is laughing at me.' Una didn't reply. The germ of an idea had begun to grow inside her head.

'Did you hear what I said? That scruffy bundle of fur you laughingly refer to as a pet is mocking me!' Una still didn't answer; her gaze was fixed on the dog. 'Una!' It was highly unusual for the reserved Englishwoman to raise her voice; she considered such outbursts unladylike.

'Yes, yes, I heard, mocking you... he just gave me an idea actually.'

'The only thing he's likely to give you is fleas!'

'Take off your clothes, Joan.'

'I beg your pardon?'

'Take off your clothes and get ready for bed. I want to see something.'

'You'll see more than you bargained for if I take off my clothes! Why don't you do it?'

'Because if I do it, I can't observe. Besides, Geraldine's nightgowns wouldn't fit me.'

'I'm going to need an explanation before I divest myself of a single item of clothing.'

'I want to picture Geraldine getting ready for bed the night she died, that's all. Call it a reconstruction of events.'

Joan thought for a moment. Una wouldn't ask her to do such a thing if it wasn't crucial to their investigations.

'Very well, I'll do it but I refuse to disrobe in front of that!' She pointed to Finn who was still standing on the bed, looking from one to the other.

'Him? Sure he couldn't care less. He's seen me in all me glory and he's still here to tell the tale.'

'Well I care. Get him out of here and I'll go along with your absurd request.'

Una scooped up the dog and tossed him into the outer room, then closed the door.

'There, happy now?'

'I'm far from happy, Una. I'm being asked to take off my clothes and re-enact the last night of a dead woman's life.'

'Don't worry, pet. If anything happens to you, I'll give you the fanciest send off Tipperary's ever seen. We'll have your wake at McCarthys and I'll get them to serve champagne and vol-au-vents. How's that?'

Joan began to laugh. 'You do realise you're totally bonkers don't you, Mrs. Murphy.'

'So I've been told, Mrs. Cahill,' grinned Una. 'More often than not by you.'

CHAPTER 10

Joan selected a full-length nightdress from Geraldine's armoire. She held it up to herself and admired her reflection in a mirror. Una humoured her friend.

'Gorgeous, Joan, suits you down to the ground.'

Joan laid it gently on the bed, then returned to the closet and took out a silk dressing gown embroidered with Geraldine's initials. Again she held it up to herself and swished from side to side, letting the silk furl around her legs.

'What do you think, Una? There are several others if you'd rather...'

'That one's ideal.' Una was growing impatient but she held her tongue, an accomplishment in itself.

Joan arranged the gown on the bed next to the nightdress. She unbuttoned her blouse slowly then removed it, taking time to fold it neatly before setting it aside. Una wasn't a patient woman at the best of times and was finding the whole rigmarole tortuous.

'For the love of God, woman. Do you always take this long to get ready for bed?'

'Of course. Why? How do you prepare to retire?'

'I tear off my clothes, throw them on a chair and jump into my pyjamas.'

Joan clucked her tongue in disapproval. Ordinarily that would have sparked an outburst from Una, but she didn't have time for quarrels.

'In your own time, pet,' she said. 'What's next?'

'Well at this point, I would remove my makeup and begin my moisturising regime.'

'Then do it.'

'There are limits to our friendship, Una Murphy. No one sees me without makeup.'

'Alright, we'll make believe you've taken off the face paint. Now what?'

Joan removed her shoes. She opened the wardrobe and placed them inside, then she unzipped her skirt and shimmied until it fell to the floor around her feet. She stepped out of it, then picked it up, folding it neatly before placing it beside her blouse. She began to remove her tights.

'This is most uncomfortable, Una. Even my late husband wasn't allowed to watch me disrobe.'

'Jayzus, really? Alright so, you can keep everything else on.'

Joan breathed a sigh of relief. She picked up the nightdress and slid it over her head, then pulled on the silk robe and wrapped it around herself, securing the belt in a neat bow. She went back to the armoir and began searching around inside.

'What are you looking for, pet?'

'Slippers. I can't walk around in bare feet.'

'Put a pair on so.'

'There aren't any in here.'

Una pushed her friend out of the way and tossed out all the shoes onto the floor. Joan was right, there were no slippers. She peered under the bed, no slippers there either.

'Get dressed, Joanie! We need to find those slippers and unless I'm very much mistaken, I know where they are.'

Joan got dressed as fast as she could. She was still buttoning her collar when Una bolted out of the room, the little terrier hot on her heels.

'Wait for me!' Joan called after her. 'Where are you going?'

'Lelia's room. I'll meet you there.'

When Joan arrived at the housekeeper's bedroom, she found her friend already searching.

'Don't just stand there,' Una told her. 'We're looking for slippers. If you find any, don't touch them.'

Finn was already on the prowl. He sniffed around the floor as he had in Geraldine's room, and his nose led him directly to the wardrobe. Una scooped him up in her arms and opened the door.

'Of course!' she said. 'Good boy, Finn. Joanie, check inside would you?' Joan peered into the dark wardrobe.

'What makes you think they'd be in here?'

'Frances mentioned them, remember? She said she threw a pair of slippers into the closet after they found Lelia.'

'She mentioned a pair of slippers. She didn't say they belonged to Lady Geraldine.'

'Just humour me, will you?'

'Here they are, I found them!' Joan used one of Lelia's shoes to pull a pair of slippers out of the wardrobe onto the floor. They were well-worn and the uppers were made from pink terry cloth.

'They can't be the ones,' said Una, disappointed. 'Lady Geraldine Hennessy wouldn't be seen dead wearing slippers like those.'

'An unfortunate choice of words, dear.'

'You know what I mean. Check again.'

'I have. Those are the only slippers in here. Maybe they're under the bed.' Joan got down on her hands and knees and looked under the housekeeper's bed. Other than a collection of dust bunnies, there was nothing. 'Lelia wasn't much of a housekeeper,' she sniffed. 'The floor under here needs a jolly good clean.' Una couldn't care less about Lelia's ability as a housekeeper.

'Bring the pink ones,' she said, 'I want to show them to Frances.'

'You bring them. I'm not touching those things.'

'Alright, well you carry Finn and I'll bring the slippers.'

Joan glanced at the dog. He was looking back at her and she could have sworn she saw him wink.

'Never mind,' she said, 'I'll bring the slippers.' She stripped a pillowcase from one the pillows and carefully captured the slippers inside it, then she followed her friend downstairs. As they neared the kitchen, they were met by the unmistakable aroma of baking. They arrived just as Frances was taking a tray of freshly-baked scones out of the oven. Joan put the pillowcase on the table and immediately went to wash her hands. Una emptied the slippers out onto the table.

'Frances,' she said, 'are these the ones you found in Lelia's room?' The cook only had to glance at them.

'Not at all, missus. The slippers I saw were brand new. Gorgeous they were, purple with gold embroidery.'

'Did you touch them?'

'I told you, I threw them into the wardrobe when the ambulance people were here.'

'Have you seen them since?'

Frances thought for a moment. 'I haven't, missus, no.'

'What do you do with your rubbish here? Do you have bins that the council collects?'

'No, Matty burns our rubbish.'

'Where?'

'At the back of the barn. He lights a fire about once a fortnight, burns the lot.'

'Has he had a fire since your mistress died?'

'I... don't think so.' Frances hesitated. 'No, definitely not.'

'Thank you. We'll leave you to get on so.'

'What should I do with these auld slippers?'

'You can throw them out.'

Una put down the dog and made her way through to the hallway. Joan and Finn followed. There was an umbrella stand just inside the front door and Una took a large golf umbrella out of it.

'Are you expecting rain?' asked Joan.

'No, I need to poke around in Matty's pile of rubbish and I don't want to touch those slippers with my hands.'

'You're obsessed with this poison business, Una. Just because so many of Agatha Christie's victims fell foul of toxins, it doesn't mean that's what happened here. Sometimes a slipper is just a slipper.'

'Just a precaution, pet. In the right hands, a slipper can also be a deadly weapon and if that's the case, I don't intend on becoming its third victim.'

CHAPTER 11

They soon found Matty's well-used burn area. A small mound of plastic bags and assorted flammable objects sat atop a pile of ash from previous fires. Una poked the bags with the tip of her umbrella, sending them cascading down through rusted cans and scorched household debris. Joan held a delicate lace handkerchief to her nose.

'Keep an eye out for anything purple,' Una told her.

'When I was invited as a guest in one of Ireland's finest country houses, I didn't imagine I'd be poking around in their rubbish.'

'Ah whisht, woman, I'm the one doing the poking.'

Even when the mound had been levelled, there was still no sign of the missing slippers.

'There's nothing else for it,' declared Una, 'we'll have to tear open every one of these bags. Where's Finn, by the way?'

'Terrorising small woodland creatures probably.'

'Good, I don't want him sniffing around here.'

The two friends went at it. They tore open bag after bag and inspected the contents before tossing them back onto the heap. Bluebottles hummed around them and the stench of rancid leftover food permeated the air. Joan's back ached and she straightened up for a moment.

'I don't remember applying for this job,' she said, 'but I'd like to tender my resignation.'

'There's only one bag to go, pet, then we're done. I must admit though, it's looking increasingly like another wild goose chase.'

'Look!' exclaimed Joan, pointing towards the woods. 'I think that horrible animal of yours has killed a chicken!'

Una had to squint in order to see. Several hundred feet away at the edge of the tree line stood Finn, and he did have something sizeable between his jaws. As always when he had something he knew he shouldn't, the little terrier stood feet akimbo, daring the two women to come and take it from him.

'Don't go after him, Joan. That's what he wants. If we chase him, he'll think it's a game. We'll never get it off him.'

'Then what should we do?'

'Ignore him. Just turn and walk towards the house.' Una raised her voice for the benefit of the dog. 'Come on, Joan, let's get a *treat* for *Finn*!'

Joan played along. 'Oh yes, *treats* for *Finn*!' Finn wasn't the smartest of his breed but he did know that when those two words came close together, it meant something tasty. He also thought he must have been a very good boy to deserve his treat so there would be plenty of praising and petting too. He dropped whatever was in his mouth and scampered in the direction of the two women as fast as his short little legs would carry him. In no time at all, he'd caught them up and Una made a grab for his collar.

'Gotcha, ya little.....!'

The minute she picked him up, Finn realised he'd been duped. He squirmed, trying to get loose, and continued his struggle until he finally realised it was fruitless.

'We'd better go and see what he killed, pet. I might have to bury it; I don't want him getting into trouble.'

'Doesn't that make you an accessory after the fact, Mrs. Murphy, not to mention perverting the course of justice.'

'Probably but ah, sure Finn's family.'

As the two friends approached the object, Una had to hold on tightly to Finn to prevent him from wriggling free. The nearer they got, the more apparent it became that it was neither a chicken nor a small woodland creature. On the ground lay a white plastic bag, covered in soil and mouldy vegetation as if Finn had found it buried somewhere in the woods.

'This could be what we're looking for!' exclaimed Una. She bent to pick up the bag but the minute she lifted it, she realised it wasn't heavy enough to contain a pair of slippers. She ripped it open anyway and inside found two large, crumpled sheets of paper. One was the decorative kind used for wrapping presents, the other plain brown shipping paper. She pulled them both out and looked inside the bag to see if there was a gift card, but found none. Although the brown sheet was incomplete, she could still make out Geraldine's name and the address of Moonbeg Manor. She couldn't see a return address but the postmark was clear. The package had been posted in Dublin.

Joan leaned over to see what her friend was looking at and Finn licked her cheek. Joan wiped away his saliva with her hand and glared at the dog. His eyes twinkled back at her.

'Detestable mutt,' she mumbled. 'I'll probably catch some foul dog disease now.' Again she leaned in to see what had Una's attention. 'Goodness!' she exclaimed. 'That could be the smoking gun, dear.'

'There's no gun as yet, pet, but I definitely smell smoke.'

'If only we could find the slippers. Perhaps they're buried in the woods too.'

Una was glad to see that Joan was finally on board. She peered into the gloom of the dense woodland. Although she knew it covered less than six acres, it might just as well have been the size of the Amazon Jungle considering their task. Then an idea popped into her head. It was a long shot, but it was better than nothing.

'Joan, take off your belt.'

'You're not going to ask me to undress again, are you?'

'No, I just need the belt.' Joan complied, relieved that at least she didn't have to take off her clothes this time. Una looped the belt under Finn's collar to create a makeshift leash, then she put him down on the ground.

'Finn!' she said, excitedly. 'Where's the toy? The *toy*, Finn, fetch the *toy*!' It was another word the dog was well-acquainted with and one which he associated with fun and games. He pounced on the plastic bag. 'No, Finn! The other toy, fetch the other *toy*!'

The terrier yanked at Joan's belt, pulling Una into the wooded undergrowth. Joan's waist was small and the belt was short, so Una had to bend low.

'Come on, Joan,' she called over her shoulder.

'I'll sit this dance out, if it's all the same with you.'

Una didn't have time to insist, she was too busy trying to stay on her feet as Finn pulled her over fallen branches. Prickly bramble bushes tore at her tights and snagged her clothes. The dog was oblivious to the thorns, his thick fur providing ample protection, and was in his element. He was a terrier after all, a Cairn terrier whose ancestors had been bred to hunt. Finn was on a mission and he knew exactly where he was going. On occasion, whenever the blackberry thickets became too dense to negotiate, she had to force him to take an alternative route, but at no time did he alter direction. Una struggled to maintain her balance as he dragged her purposefully through the undergrowth. Once or twice he stopped briefly to sniff a shrub, or water it, but otherwise he was resolute.

Finally, at the base of a huge hawthorn bush, he made the discovery Una had been hoping for. A partially-buried, white plastic bag was poking out of the soil. She picked up the dog before he had a chance to tear the bag asunder and possibly harm himself in the process. She peered inside and saw the unmistakable glint of gilt against royal purple. Bingo! She'd found the gun, or rather Finn had. She shook off the soil and debris and, with her dog tucked under one arm, retraced their steps back through the wood.

CHAPTER 12

'I can't wait to tell the Monsignor when he gets back!'

'Oh no you don't, Joan. We're not telling Terrence anything.'

'Why on earth not?'

'Because we don't know what we have yet. There's just no point in involving him at this stage.'

'Very well, you're the boss... apparently.'

'That's right. Now pull up your big girl pants, we have work to do. First things first, we'll need rubber gloves. We can't afford to take any chances. I'll borrow a pair from Frances.'

The two friends began making their way back towards the house. The clear blue skies and warmth of the early July sunshine were a welcome respite from the all-too-often dreary Irish weather. Joan raised her face to the sun.

'Couldn't we sit outside for a while, Una? Just for a little while to enjoy the sunshine?'

'If you like, pet, I don't suppose there's any desperate rush. You'll ruin that porcelain complexion of yours though.'

'You're right, dear. I'll go up and get my sunhat.'

'I'll drop these things off in my room and get the rubber gloves. I'll meet you in the garden.'

They entered the house together and while Joan headed straight upstairs, Una stood for a few moments in the hall, allowing her eyes to adjust to the relative gloom. She popped the umbrella back into its stand by the door. Finn was off his lead now and trying to decide whether he should stay with the calm human who fed him or go and torment the highly-strung one who was climbing the stairs. Una limped off to the kitchen and he followed. Her old joints weren't accustomed to cavorting through woodland. Frances wasn't there so Una picked up a pair of yellow Marigold gloves she found beside the sink and returned to the entrance hall. There was a deep ache in her hip now so she climbed the steps slowly. Finn ran ahead, then hesitated and ran back to her. Una waved him away.

'Go 'way outta that! You'll have me over.'

Joan looked down at her friend from the top of the staircase, a wide-brimmed sunhat in her hand.

'That hip of yours bothering you again, dear?'

'It wasn't too bad 'til me laddo here dragged me through the woods at breakneck speed.'

'Ah, we're not as young as we were, Una,' commiserated Joan as she began to descend the stairs.

'I don't need you to remind me, thanks. I have an arthritic hip to do that.'

'Be careful it doesn't give out on you. You should use a walking stick.'

Una stopped in her tracks and glared up at her friend.

'I will in me hole! Isn't it bad enough I'm hobbling around like an auld biddy? I don't need a purpose-made accessory to advertise me failing body to the world.'

'Lady Geraldine used a stick. I saw a gorgeous antique one beside her bed.'

'She was an old lady.'

'She was two years older than you, dear, three years older than me.'

'Typical! Whenever you bring up age, you have to remind me I'm the older one. Why don't you go the whole hog and tell me that losing weight would help?' Una wasn't really angry with Joan, she was angry that her body was letting her down but, true to human nature, she was taking it out on the one closest to her.

'I would never say such a thing to you.'

'No, but you think it.'

'So you can read my mind, can you? Tell me, what am I thinking now?'

Una face broke into a grin. 'You're wondering whether or not you should push me down these stairs.'

'It's a miracle,' exclaimed Joan. 'She's a mind reader after all!' The two women grabbed each other's hand as they passed on the stairs. The storm clouds had parted and the sun shone through once more.

Finn watched intently as Una stashed the bags under her bed. He was a staunch advocate of the 'finders keepers' concept and as he had discovered the bags, surely they belonged to him.

'Don't even think about it,' warned Una. She knew she needed to distract him, take his mind off the plastic bags, so she called his name in an excited voice. He immediately came to attention. 'Will we go for a *walk*?' He began to leap around excitedly. He'd heard that all-important word and nothing else now mattered.

Una closed the bedroom door behind her but not before she'd grabbed her hat. It was an old felt affair that had seen better days. The once deep-green material had long since faded to an insipid shade of sage, and the colorful silk flowers that encircled the crown now looked as if they'd come from last week's supermarket bouquet. Finn shadowed her as she crossed the landing. Her hip nagged with every step.

'Jesus,' she grumbled aloud. 'I wouldn't mind this getting old business if it wasn't so bloody painful!'

She didn't stop at the stairs but carried on to Geraldine's room. She was looking for the walking stick Joan had mentioned and she found it propped up against the wall beside the bed. It had a silver top and the shaft was made from highly-polished black wood. She lifted it. It was much lighter than she expected. She held it in her hand and considered putting it back where she found it, then made up her mind.

'Well,' she told Finn, 'I don't suppose I'll ever hear the last of this from Joan Cahill but feck it.' She tried it out and it took a few steps for her to get used to the stick, but in no time at all she was limping along nicely. 'There now,' she said, 'I should have got meself one of these yokes long ago.' The dog looked at his mistress as if he understood.

She joined Joan in the garden and either Joan hadn't noticed the walking stick or she was too polite to mention it. Una suspected the latter. She sat opposite her, parking her ample backside on one of four white wooden chairs arranged around a matching table.

'Well? Aren't you going to say anything?' Joan sensed her friend was spoiling for another set-to.

'Aren't the roses lovely?' she said.

'I meant about me using the stick.'

'I wonder what they use to control the aphids here. I have frightful problems with them at home.' She clearly wasn't biting today so Una gave it up as a bad job.

'A cuppa would be nice. Did you ask Frances to make us a pot?'

'I did, dear, she'll be out in a minute.' No sooner had Joan uttered the words than they saw the cook coming across the garden towards them carrying a tea tray. As well as the teapot and cups, there were fresh scones and butter, strawberry jam and a little pot of clotted cream.

'Grand day,' remarked Frances cheerily as she placed the tray on the table.

'Gorgeous altogether,' agreed Una.

'Would you like me to pour, missus?'

'No thank you, Frances, we can manage.' Frances left the two old ladies to help themselves and disappeared back inside the house.

'Are we still not telling Terrence what we found?' Joan was hoping Una had changed her mind.

'Not yet, no. After dinner tonight you and I will go to my room and we'll inspect those slippers more closely.'

Joan poured the tea. Una stirred hers and gazed into the swirling vortex it created. She remembered doing the same thing once before. It had helped her solve the bog body case and she hoped it might inspire her again. She allowed herself to be drawn into the hypnotic little whirlpool.

'You've very quiet,' said Joan, after several minutes. 'I haven't upset you again, have I?'

'No, no, pet, not at all. I was just thinking, that's all.'

'What were you thinking about?'

'The break in. Why was the barn broken into if nothing was stolen? Don't you find that odd?' Joan knew Una's questions were rhetorical, that she was just thinking aloud.

'Oh forget about that for now,' she said. 'It's a glorious day, let's just enjoy our lovely cream tea in these beautiful surroundings.' She sliced a scone in half. 'Now, dear, do you prefer your clotted cream on top of your jam like they do it in Cornwall, or the jam on top of the cream like they have it in Devon.'

'Sure it all goes down the same hole. What difference does it make?'

'It makes a great deal of difference if you're from Devon or Cornwall.'

'You English are quare yokes. If that's all you've have had to worry about for the last thousand years, ye haven't done too bad!'

CHAPTER 13

When Frances came to collect the tray, she said Terrence had phoned.

'He won't be back today,' she told them. 'He'll be tied up with the Archbishop for a while longer, so it's just the two of ye for dinner.'

'What about Matty?' asked Joan.

'When Matty goes to Fethard, missus, there's no telling when he'll be back. Knowing him, he'll be in McCarthys on the lash. Will ye eat out here, ladies, or will I set the dinner table?'

'Thank you, Frances,' replied Una, 'your scones have taken the edge off our appetite. We'll eat later if that's alright with you.'

The cook inclined her head in acknowledgement and retreated back inside the house.

'Excellent!' said Una. 'No men around to get in our way.'

'And I don't have to watch that big oaf eat,' grinned Joan. 'We couldn't have arranged it better ourselves!' She offered up her palm to her friend.

'What in God's name are you doing, woman?'

'High five, Una!'

'We'll have none of that malarkey! What are you, a Yank? I don't know what the world is coming to with all these creeping Americanisms. You'll be saying 'my bad' or 'from the get-go' next, or talking about ice boxes and fanny packs.'

Joan clapped her hand over her mouth at Una's final example of a creeping Americanism, but a blurted laugh escaped despite all attempts to suppress it. Una began to giggle too which made Joan laugh even more. On hearing the commotion, Finn poked his head out from behind a large hydrangea shrub to see what was going on. He was panting. His mouth was open and his lips pulled back as far as they would go. His tongue lolled out to one side. Una recognised the face of mischief and knew instinctively that her dog was up to no good.

'What are you doing in there?' she scolded. 'Come here this minute!' The terrier disappeared back inside the shrubbery, then reappeared, his jaws shut tightly around something.

'What's he got in his mouth this time?' said Joan.

'A snail probably.'

'Ugh, disgusting creature!'

Una felt the need to justify his actions. Although he might be a disgusting creature, Finn was her disgusting creature.

'The French eat snails,' she reminded her friend.

'I rest my case,' came Joan's haughty reply.

Finn knew he was the object of their attention and saw it as a green light for mischief. He ran around the two old ladies, dodging in and out between the legs of their chairs.

'Ignore him, Joan, he'll tire himself out eventually.' Ignoring Finn was easier said than done, but finally their patience paid off and he began to calm down. He approached Joan and put his two front paws up on her knees. He looked into her face with a bright-eyed intent that Joan mistook for affection.

'I have to admit,' she said, cautiously patting his scruffy head, 'you are a handsome little fellow.' In appreciation of the compliment, Finn spat a half-chewed snail into her lap. Joan screamed and leapt to her feet. She flicked the semi-masticated mollusk off her skirt.

'He did that on purpose!' she exclaimed. 'Now I'm going to have to change my clothes!' She turned on her heel and stormed off towards the house. As soon as Joan vacated her chair, the dog jumped up and took her place. Una grinned at him across the table.

'Good boy,' she whispered. He wagged his tail.

Una gave her friend ten minutes or so to cool down before she returned to the house. She began to climb the stairs with the help of Geraldine's silver-topped walking cane. She was pleased with her decision to use it and grateful for the relief it gave her.

Once safely ensconced in her room, she donned the yellow rubber gloves and pulled out both bags from underneath the bed. She put on her reading glasses and took out the two sheets of wrapping paper. She studied the brown one. The Dublin postmark intrigued her. She put it aside and very carefully removed the slippers from the second bag. She sat on the bed and put one of them flat on the palm of her hand.

Holding it up to the light, she turned it this way and that. It was clearly an expensive item. The material used was of superior quality and the stitching and embroidery had been professionally executed. She put it down and picked up the other one. Again she laid it flat on her hand and began her inspection. It was just as beautifully made as the first and it wasn't until Una looked inside that she found a slight anomaly. At the heel, where the insole ended, the stitching looked as if it had been unpicked then sewn back together in a less skilful manner. She took off her glasses and held them nearer the slipper, using one of the lenses as a magnifying glass. Just then, there was a quiet tap on her door and Joan let herself in.

'Found anything, dear?' she enquired.

'I don't want to speak too soon, Joanie, but I think we could be looking at our murder weapon.'

'A slipper?'

'Do me a favour would you, pet?' Get me your manicure set.'

'I hardly think this is any time to be doing your nails!'

'It's not for my nails. I need to do little surgery on this slipper.'

'Be careful, Una! Don't you think it's time we called the Guards?'

'No, I don't!' Una was adamant. 'We don't want that shower of eejits running amok with our case just when we might be getting somewhere. Besides, as far as they're concerned there's been no crime committed.'

Joan returned a few minutes later with her manicure set and a small sewing kit. Una's reading glasses were perched precariously on the end of her nose.

'Give me something to remove these stitches,' she said, holding out her hand like a doctor about to perform an operation. Joan passed her a small tool designed specifically to remove stitches, open seams and cut threads. Una eyed it suspiciously.

'A small pair of scissors would suffice,' she said, flatly.

'I'm sure a broken bottle would suffice,' replied Joan, 'but that seam ripper is the right tool for the job.'

Una shot her an acid glance. She knew Joan was right but she wasn't about to admit it, not out loud anyway. She set about opening the extraneous stitches, one by one. When they'd all been cut, she pushed her finger into the aperture and tried to peer inside. It was impossible.

'Now I do need the scissors,' she said. Joan handed her a pair of dainty cuticle scissors and Una inserted them into the slit. She opened it carefully, like a surgeon opening an incision with a retractor.

'There's definitely something in here, pet. Have you any tweezers in that kit of yours?'

'Of course, dear, here you are.'

Using Joan's tweezers, Una managed to grip whatever had been secreted inside the makeshift hiding place, but no matter how hard she twisted and pulled, she couldn't free it. After several minutes of listening to her friend cursing and blaspheming, Joan ran out of patience.

'Oh for goodness sake,' she snapped, 'let me do it! Una was so taken aback by her friend's assertive command that she immediately took off the gloves and gave them to her. She handed her the scissors and in no time, Joan had the seam between the inner and outer sole completely unfastened. She opened up the slipper like a clam.

'There!' she announced.

'What's that?'

What appeared to be a clear plastic disk, about an inch in diameter, had been stuck to the underside of the insole. Joan worked it loose with the tweezers and held it up to the light.

'There seems to be a tiny amount of liquid in it, dear.'

'Here, give me those gloves!' Once Una's hands were protected, she inspected the object more closely. 'It looks to me like two plastic disks have been somehow welded together to form a bladder of sorts.' She turned it over. 'The top disk is slightly more rigid and I can see a needle in the centre of it, like a tiny hypodermic. That must be what was keeping it from coming loose.'

'Una!' Joan's tone was one of urgency. She realised they were looking at what could quite conceivably be a deadly instrument of murder. 'We're in completely over our heads here.'

'I'll bet it's a poison of some sort,' mused Una, ignoring her friend. 'I'd love to know what exactly.'

'That's a job for the authorities. Una, we need to call the police.'

'Hmmm... I just want to take a wee look in the barn first.'

'Alright, but then we call the police.'

Una didn't answer. The bottom drawer of her bedside table was empty so she stashed the disk inside it, picked up the silver-topped walking stick and headed downstairs. Finn followed her. Joan sighed with exasperation and did the same.

CHAPTER 14

Joan caught up with them just as they
entered the barn. Dual-aspect windows
made the interior surprisingly light and airy
for an outbuilding and sunlight streamed in
to reveal an array of tools and gadgets
hanging neatly around the walls, everything
necessary to maintain Moonbeg Manor and
its demesne. A large, ride-on mower was
parked just inside the door and, judging by
the condition of its bright red paintwork, it
was brand new. Una gave a long, low
whistle.

'The equipment in here must be worth
thousands. Why would anyone go to the
trouble of breaking in, just to leave empty-
handed?'

Joan shook her head. 'It doesn't make
sense. Thieves who target isolated rural
houses like this generally take everything of

value, power tools especially. I've read about it in the papers. Perhaps they were disturbed.'

Una wasn't buying into Joan's theory. 'No, that's not it. Something about this stinks.'

'Well whatever it is, I think your dog can smell it. Look.'

Una followed Joan's gaze over to a door where a brass sign overhead read TACK ROOM. The little terrier had his rear end in the air and his nose pressed to the gap at the bottom. He'd picked up a compelling scent and deep sniffs alternated with loud snorts. Una tried to pull him away but Finn was going nowhere. He began scratching furiously at the gap, then stopped to whimper pitifully at his mistress. She opened the door for him, just a crack, but it was enough for Finn to squeeze through. Joan gave her friend a gentle nudge from behind and, as Una pushed open the door, a ray of sunlight streamed in from the barn. Particles of dust swirled around inside it.

The faint aromas of leather, saddle soap and neatsfoot oil hung in the air and cobwebs laced the rafters and walls. A string hung down from a light fixture and Joan pulled it. Instantly, the small room was bathed in a harsh incandescent glow. Bridles, girth straps and covered saddles hung on racks around the walls, all thick with dust. Finn homed in on one particular saddle and stood on his hind legs, like a meerkat on sentry duty, sniffing and snorted at its cover. Una watched him with interest. She trusted her dog's nose better than she trusted her own eyes.

'Can you see anything different about that one, Joan?'

'No, they all look the same to me. This place could do with a good clean.'

'But they're not all the same. Look. The other covers have an even layer of dust on them. The one Finn picked out only has it at the front, and there's a ridge of dust across the middle. Someone has turned the saddle cover over on itself. See?'

'Well, yes, now you come to mention it. But what does it mean?'

'I don't know, pet, I don't know. But I intend to find out.'

She flipped over the cover, exposing the rear of the saddle. A small brass nameplate was riveted to the cantle. Her reading glasses hung on a string around her neck and she put them on. She leaned in to decipher the name. It read TERRENCE McCARTHY. Joan saw it at the same time.

'Perhaps he came to check it,' she said, 'after he heard the place had been broken into.'

Una was more suspicious by nature than her friend and didn't respond. Instead she inspected the saddle inch by inch, running her fingers over the leather until, finally, she straightened up.

'Would you ever go and get me that manicure set again, Joan? I think I've found something.'

Joan set off immediately. 'Don't forget the rubber gloves,' Una called after her, 'and bring one of those little self-seal sandwich bags from the kitchen!'

She took off her glasses and, as before, used them as a magnifying lens. She moved them in and out until she had the tiny needle tip in focus. 'Jesus, Mary and Joseph,' she said to herself, 'if ever you'd used this saddle, Terrence McCarthy, you'd be having dinner with God tonight instead of the Archbishop.'

When Joan arrived back with the items, Una pulled on the rubber gloves.

'Be careful,' Joan told her.

It took fifteen minutes or so to tease away the leather from the small bladder. It should have taken longer but whoever had fixed it in place used superglue and the well-oiled leather had resisted the cyanoacrylate, preventing it from adhering properly. Una dislodged the bladder with the tweezers and, when her friend opened the plastic sandwich bag, she dropped it inside.

'Joan,' she announced, 'it's time to call Chief Inspector Quinn.'

'Oh thank God! I'm so glad you've finally seen sense. Won't Gerard be surprised and delighted to hear from us again!'

'He'll be surprised alright. I doubt very much if he'll be delighted. This will be the second time we've been one step ahead of the Guards.'

'Does this mean we can go home now, dear?'

'Not yet. We have to kill Terrence first.'

'I beg your pardon?'

'Well someone is clearly trying to. We have to make whoever it is think that they've succeeded.'

'Oh dear, poor Terrence.'

'Never mind that now. Come on, pet, help me put everything back the way we found it.'

*

Una made a call from her room to Chief Inspector Quinn.

'I'm being redirected,' she whispered to Joan. 'Apparently he's temporarily stationed down in Cork.'

The Inspector was sitting in his office pouring over a ten-year-old case for the umpteenth time when the phone rang.

'Una Murphy? Put her through.' He barely gave her time to dispense with the pleasantries before he enquired about Aine.

'She's grand, thanks for asking. Still at Trinity, of course, graduates next year. She's hoping to get a job in the prosecutor's office.'

'The prosecutor's office? But I thought she wanted to be a defense attorney.'

'She does. Aine says that to be a good defense attorney, you have to study the tactics of a prosecutor.'

'Fair play to her. Well at least it means we'll be on the same side of the bench, for a while at least. Now what can I do for you, Mrs. Murphy?'

'Are you busy, Gerard?'

'Well if you call pissing in the wind busy, then yes.'

'How would you like me to hand you a nice juicy murder on a plate?' There was a long silence. 'Gerard?' Una shook the receiver. 'Hello. Are you still there?'

'Yes, I'm still here. Who is the unfortunate victim this time?'

'Well actually there are two, in Tipperary anyway. There could be a third in South Africa, plus an attempted murder here.'

The Inspector rolled his eyes. 'You have been busy, haven't you. I suppose you have evidence to support these claims?'

'I have the murder weapon.' There was another long silence. Again, Una shook the receiver. 'I think we must have a bad line,' she told Joan. 'Can you still hear me, Gerard?'

'I can hear you. So tell me, what kind of murder weapon is it? A gun? A knife?'

'Nothing as commonplace as that. It's genius. Wait 'til you see it!'

Gerard didn't know what to think. He couldn't bring himself to dismiss Una Murphy's claims as the ravings of a mad woman. After all, she had single-handedly solved the bog body case in Ballyanny. He knew her to be a sharp and intuitive woman but coming out of the blue, her allegations seemed incredulous.

'You wouldn't be pulling my leg by any chance would you, Mrs. Murphy?'

'Chief Inspector, if you think I have nothing better to do than make hoax phone calls to the police, you can get back to pissing in the wind. I'll find someone who will take me seriously.'

'Alright, alright. When can we meet?'

'We'll be in McCarthys Bar in Fethard tomorrow at noon. You can buy us lunch.'

CHAPTER 15

Una woke to the sound of the front door being slammed shut. She switched on the bedside light and peered at her watch. It was half two in the morning. She listened as heavy footsteps mounted the stairs, followed by a bedroom door clicking shut. She switched off the light, settled back down and pulled the covers up to her chin.

It was almost half eight when she arrived downstairs. The night before, they had agreed to take breakfast in the kitchen and Joan was already sipping tea and swapping lemon drizzle recipes with the cook. When Una appeared, she told her that they were thinking of having a competition to determine whose was the better cake, but Una had other things on her mind. She poured herself a cup of tea from the pot and stirred it, staring blankly into the little whirlpool.

The break-in. That had to be the key. If only she could find out who'd broken into the barn, she was sure she'd have her perpetrator.

'Frances,' she said. 'would you mind bringing me the phone please. And is there a telephone directory I could use?'

'There is o'course.' The cook jumped up from her seat. 'I'll just be a minute.'

'Who are you going to call?' enquired Joan.

'Ghostbusters,' replied Una, sarcastically.

'Oh, you're in that kind of mood this morning are you?'

Frances brought the phone and directory, then began preparing breakfast. Una put on her reading glasses and started thumbing through the pages.

'So are you going to tell me who you're calling or not?' said Joan.

'If you must know, I'm ringing round all the local bed and breakfast places.'

'What for? Are we leaving?'

Una shook her head. She began dialing and when Joan opened her mouth to ask another question, Una put her finger to her lips.

'Abbey View? Yes, hello. I'm enquiring whether you've had a guest stay recently with a South African accent.' There was a pause. 'That's right, a South African, male or female. It would have been somewhere around the fourteenth of June.' There was another pause while the person on the other end enquired as to the caller's identity.

Una hesitated. 'I represent the.... Department of Health,' she said. 'We have reason to believe this person contracted an infectious disease and has unwittingly brought it into the country.' Again there was a pause as another question was asked. 'No, not the Ebola virus.' No sense in causing mass panic. 'It's....er... it's known as Baboon Pox. No, it's not fatal. What's that? Symptoms? Well, a skin rash is usually the first sign... and a fever. The cure?' Una glanced at a fruit bowl on the table. 'Bananas,' she said. Joan's eyes widened and Una shrugged helplessly. 'Yes, that's right, bananas. They help prevent contracting the disease and they cure it too. They're a counteracting agent.'

What Una didn't realise was that she was about to become responsible for a total depletion of Tipperary's banana stocks. In a matter of days, not a single banana could be bought east of the River Suir. The tin foil

142

hat brigade enjoyed a large representation in rural Ireland and rumours such as this were like manna from heaven for conspiracists.

'No? Then I'm sorry to have troubled you. By the way, could I ask that you treat this call as confidential?' By making the request, Una had guaranteed that every minute detail of their conversation would be county-wide within the hour.

'Baboon Pox?' scoffed Joan. 'Is that the best you could come up with?'

'In the time available, yes. How about you make the next call and I ridicule you?'

Joan held up her hands in mock surrender. 'No, you carry on, dear. You're doing a splendid job.'

The same telephone conversation was repeated four or five times, each one resulting in a negative response. When Una called the next number, she was surprised to find the owner had been expecting her call and was already in a state of panic. It appeared rumours spread rapidly amongst the B&B community.

'I see,' said Una, winking at Joan, 'well, that's very interesting. And the guest's name was...?' She scribbled something in the corner of the directory. Thanks a million for your help and... What's that now? Ah try not to worry, we think it's only in the incubation stage. I'd advise you to eat three or four bananas a day for the next few days and you'll be grand. Yes, thank you, goodbye now, bu-bye, bye byebyebye... no, it's no trouble at all, you're very welcome, yes, bu-bye, mind yourself now, byebyebyebye.'

Una hung up the phone. 'Bingo!' she exclaimed.

'So who is it?' asked Joan excitedly.

Una took a gulp of her now tepid tea. She ripped off the corner of the page she'd written on and hurried out of the kitchen with it.

'You're infuriating!' Joan called after her.

Una almost collided with Terrence in the doorway. She barged past him and he looked after her for a moment, then came through into the kitchen. His hair was in disarray and his eyelids were set at half-mast. He sat at the table opposite Joan.

'Goodness,' she said, 'you look a little the worse for wear if you don't mind me saying so.'

He sneered at her. 'I do mind as is happens, Mrs. Murphy, and I'm sure that I look a damn sight better than you do!'

'Are you drunk, Monsignor? That's very unkind and I'm Joan, remember?'

Terrence laughed out loud, then winced and put his hand to his head. 'My apologies, Joan, I had a few drinks on the way back last night. My head feels like a burst mattress.'

Frances poured him a cup of tea. 'Will I scramble you some eggs, Father?' she asked.

He pushed the cup away. 'No eggs, just black coffee and some paracetamol.'

In no time at all Frances had delivered a mug of steaming hot coffee and two caplets. He threw the tablets into his mouth and took a gulp of the hot coffee, then spluttered it all out over the table.

'For feck's sake!' he yelled. 'Get me a glass of water, woman!'

Joan was appalled by the priest's bullish behaviour, hangover or no hangover, but she decided not to pursue it while he was still suffering the aftereffects of his drinking binge. Frances rushed to fill a tumbler under the tap and Joan attempted to strike up a conversation.

'It must have been a long day for you yesterday.'

'What's that supposed to mean?' he barked.

'Goodness me, Terrence, there's no need to bite my head off! I merely assumed that because you didn't return until the early hours of the morning, you must have had a long day.'

Terrence looked penitent. 'You really will have to forgive me this morning, Joan. You're right, it was a long day and a very stressful one.'

Frances mopped up the mess off the table and brought him two more caplets. He tossed them to the back of his mouth and took a gulp of water, then put his elbows on the table and buried his face in his hands. Joan made another attempt to cheer him up.

'Well I have some good news for you,' she said. 'While you were busy with the Archbishop, we discovered who the murderer is.'

Terrence lifted his face from his hands and levered up an eyelid, trying to focus on the Englishwoman.

'What did you say?'

'We found out who committed the murders.'

'And?'

'Well I don't actually know who it is, but Una does.'

'Una knows a lot of things,' came a voice from the doorway. The old woman had returned unnoticed and was standing in the shadows, leaning on the walking stick. Terrence turned and looked at her.

'Nice stick,' he said, turning back.

'It's your aunt's, I borrowed it. Do you mind?'

'You can keep it for all I care. Joan tells me you found something out yesterday.'

'That's right. While you were out doing God's work, Joan and I were busy investigating, Finn too.' She looked around. 'Where is he by the way?'

'He was here a minute ago,' replied Joan. 'Don't worry, dear, I expect he'll turn up. Come and sit down.'

Una sat next to the priest. 'God Almighty, you stink of alcohol. Good night, was it?'

'I had one or two, what's it to you?'

'Jayzus, someone got out of bed the wrong side this morning. I don't care if you drink yourself into oblivion, but what if you'd been stopped by the Guards? It could have cost you your licence.'

'In case it has escaped your notice, Mrs. Murphy, I hold one of the highest ranks in the Catholic Church. I could kick the Commissioner of An Garda Síochána in the bollocks and he'd ask if my foot was hurt. Now kindly tell me what it is that you found out yesterday.'

'No!'

'No?'

'Not until you stop behaving like a badger with a sore arse. Now go and take a shower, you're taking me and Joan to McCarthys for lunch.'

'Take yourselves. I'm going back to bed.' Terrence's face was in his hands again.

'Suit yourself. We'll pack up our things and go home so, but when the killer makes another attempt on your life, we won't be here to protect you.' The priest's head shot up. There are few things more effective in curing a hangover than a mortal threat.

'What do you mean another attempt?'

'If you snap out of that bad mood, I might tell you.'

'Alright, alright,' he said, pulling himself up out of his chair. 'I'm going to my room to take a shower.'

'Good. See if you can scrub off some of that attitude while you're at it.'

CHAPTER 16

It was half eleven when Terrence came
bounding down the stairs. His hair was still
wet but he'd slicked it back neatly and was
wearing his clerical vestments. Una and
Joan sat waiting in the hallway. He gave
them a rueful smile.

'I thought I'd wear my official robes,' he
said, 'that way we're guaranteed a table.
McCarthys can get fierce busy during the
tourist season.' Una looked him up and
down.

'Well you look a sight better than you did
earlier.'

'I might be a member of the clergy, but
first and foremost I'm an Irishman. It takes
more than a few snorts of Tullamore Dew
to keep me down. Holy and hardy, that's
me.'

'And totally unencumbered by false modesty,' remarked Joan.

Terrence hesitated momentarily while he processed Joan's comment, then he threw his head back and laughed heartily.

'So are you ladies going to tell me about this revelation of yours or do I have to find out who wants me dead the hard way?'

'I'll tell you,' replied Una, 'in my own good time.' The smile slid from his face and he fixed his gaze on her.

'You won't wait 'til it's too late, will you Mrs. Murphy.'

Una returned his gaze. 'Don't worry, I have a plan. People who commit crimes like this are like terrorists who plant bombs. They're cowards. They lurk in the shadows and wait. Did you ever go on a grouse shoot, Terrence?'

'I've been on a few. Why?'

'Think of this as a grouse hunt. We have to flush the bird out into the open from its cover so we can see it.' She checked her watch. 'We'd better get going or we'll be late.'

'Late for what?'

'We're meeting someone.'

'Who?'

'Someone you owe an apology to.'

'Do you have to be so bloody cryptic all the time?'

'All will become clear in due course, Monsignor.'

It was a beautiful day and the short drive into Fethard was postcard perfect. The country lane meandered alongside fields which had been ploughed and grazed for centuries but hadn't changed shape since Medieval times. Dark green hedges lined the road and, at intervals, opened up to reveal pastures where cows and sheep grazed contentedly. Beech trees bowed their branches overhead to form sun-dappled canopies, and wild flowers of every hue dotted the hedgerows. It was an idyllic landscape to enchant even the most jaded of tourists, but today the beauty of their surroundings only served to magnify the serious business at hand. All three occupants of the car remained silent, looking out of the windows without seeing.

The small town of Fethard was on a hill. It was always crowded on warm, summer days and today was no exception. As usual, tourists outnumbered locals. The Americans were easily identifiable. Their clothes looked new and colourful, rendering the locals somewhat drab in comparison. Most had come to the land their ancestors had left behind and they'd chosen their travel apparel carefully. For many, their visit was a pilgrimage of sorts and, subconsciously perhaps, they wanted to impress the spirit of their forefathers.

The once-walled town had been built when the Anglo-Normans arrived in Ireland eight centuries before and was famous for its ruins. Visitors strolled through narrow streets in groups of two and three, capturing images with their smart phones and cameras. Terrence had to slam on the brakes as a tourist dressed in shorts backed blindly into the road to photograph a traditional old shop front.

'Look at yer man,' growled Terrence. 'English by the look of those lily-white legs. I'm surprised some of these people live as long as they do. Listen, why don't you two get out here? I'll find a place to park and meet you in McCarthys.'

'Good idea,' agreed Una. 'The least distance I have to walk the better.'

'You should have brought that walking stick,' reproached Joan.

'Using it in the house is one thing,' Una told her, 'I'd rather crawl than be seen out with a stick.'

When the two friends arrived at McCarthys, they found a mass of people swarming around the entrance. Una wasn't at all surprised. Since 1840 the McCarthy family had been promising to 'wine you, dine you and bury you' and their establishment was legendary. It had remained virtually unchanged for over a century and visitors came from far and wide to experience its authentic ambiance.

'I doubt we'll even get inside,' said Joan, 'never mind secure a table.'

Just then a police car screeched to a halt outside the bar, blue lights flashing, and the tightly-packed crowd craned its collective neck to see what the fuss was about. The front passenger door opened and a man in a wrinkled navy blue suit got out. As the car pulled away, Una realised it was Chief Inspector Gerard Quinn. She grabbed Joan and the two friends made their way towards him. He smiled when he spotted them.

'Well, ladies, how's things? Jesus, is the Pope lunching here today? I had to park outside town and call for a patrol car to drive me in.'

He surveyed the assembled crowd and realised that all eyes were still on him. The previously raucous mob were now murmuring amongst themselves, waiting for something to happen. It gave him an idea. He pulled out his An Garda Síochána badge from his jacket pocket and held it aloft.

'Police business!' he shouted. The crowd became silent. 'Stand aside now! Police business!'

He positioned himself between the two elderly women and led them through the throng towards the entrance. Once there, he flashed the badge at a young redhead who seemed to be in control of admission.

'We need a table,' he told her in an authoritative tone. The young woman gave his badge a cursory glance, but the stoic expression on her freckled face remained unchanged.

'Two hours,' she said, flatly.

'Young lady,' he said, 'I am Chief Inspector Quinn and I'm here on official police business.'

'I don't give a fiddler's fart who y'are. It's still two hours.'

He pulled back his jacket slightly to reveal a snub-nosed thirty-eight tucked into his belt. The girl glanced at it.

'And here was me thinking you were just pleased to see me,' she sneered, holding his gaze. She clearly wasn't in the slightest bit intimidated and as Gerard's ruse was a pretense anyway, he decided not to push his luck.

'Looks like we'll have to wait,' he told his two lunch guests. They didn't have to wait long.

Terrence came jogging down the street, his long black cassock furling about his legs. As he approached, the crowd moved back. It was like watching Moses part the Red Sea. He slowed to a walk and made his way through to the entrance unimpeded.

'Rosie!' He greeted the freckled-faced redhead on the door like an old friend. 'My second favourite Irish woman after Maureen O'Hara.'

The girl's sour demeanour brightened considerably.

'Well, Father! I didn't think we'd see you again so soon.'

'Ah sure I only had a few scoops last night; I've come for a top-up.' The two of them laughed and Terrence introduced his luncheon party.

'These are two very good friends of mine, Rosie, Mrs. Murphy and Mrs. Cahill.' The redhead nodded at each. He motioned towards Gerard. 'And this is......'

'Chief Inspector Quinn,' prompted Una.

The girl gave Gerard a contemptuous glance. 'We've met,' she said, curling her lip.

'Now then, me darlin',' continued Terrence, 'we need a table. The snug would be perfect if it's available.'

'No bother. Give me a minute or two. I have to throw out... I mean I have to move some people around.'

'You're a star, Rosie.' She hurried away.

Gerard exhaled audibly. 'She's a hard nut to crack,' he said.

'Rosie's alright when you get to know her,' laughed Terrence. 'Mind, you wouldn't want to get on the wrong side of her. I've seen her throw drunks twice her size out of here.'

'Noted.'

They heard a commotion inside the bar and Rosie reappeared, escorting two middle-aged couples out onto the street.

'Well I nevah....,' protested an English woman with an upper-class accent.

'Bye now,' said Rose cheerily. 'Be sure and give us a good review on Trip Advisor!' The couples left reluctantly. 'Two minutes, Father, they're just clearing your table.'

Una smirked at Terrence. 'So you stopped here on the way home last night?'

'What if I did?' He looked at Gerard. 'It's not against the law is it, Chief Inspector?'

'Not yet, thank God.'

Murder at the Big House

CHAPTER 17

The bar buzzed with the chatter of holidaymakers. Every table was occupied, most with more than one party, and waitresses moved nimbly between them. Keeping up with the lunch trade was like keeping plates spinning on sticks. Una instantly regretted her choice of venue. How on earth would they be able to talk if they couldn't even hear themselves think? Rosie saved the day. She escorted them to a cosy snug at the back, a small wood-panelled cubicle far enough away from the crowded restaurant to muffle the din.

The room was dimly lit by a single lamp. A settle against the wall provided seating at one edge of an oblong table and Una sidled onto it. She scooted her ample posterior along the seat and Joan followed her in. The two men sat on chairs opposite.

'Aisling will be yer waitress today,' announced Rosie. She winked at Terrence and left.

'That wan is some bold hussy,' grumbled Una.

'Rosie's a meeter and greeter,' grinned Terrence. 'It's her job to be friendly.'

'Meeter and greeter, is it? Bouncer more like, and I didn't notice her being friendly to anyone else!' Una scowled at Gerard who had been fidgeting ever since they sat down. He wasn't there to listen to small talk, he wanted to get down to the purpose of the meeting. She addressed him as she would an errant pupil.

'For the love of God, Inspector, would you ever sit still? You're making me nervous.' Just then, a flustered young woman came in. She took a small notepad and pencil from her apron pocket and flipped back an errant lock of blonde hair that had fallen into her eyes.

'What can I get ye to drink?' she asked.

'Tea for me,' replied Una.

'Me too please, dear,' added Joan.

'I'm on duty,' said Gerard. 'You'd better make that three teas.'

'And what about yourself, Father,' enquired Aisling.

'I'll have a pint. Hair of the dog.'

'Give him a whiskey chaser with that,' Una instructed the blonde. 'Make it a double.' The others looked at her in surprise. 'Eat, drink and be merry,' she said, 'for tomorrow you die.'

There was no point in beginning their meeting when the waitress's return was imminent, but they didn't have to wait long. Within minutes, Aisling had arrived back carrying a tray. On it was a large pot of tea, three cups and saucers, a pint of Guinness and a large glass of Tullamore Dew. Gerard was back to fidgeting. Una cast him a stern glance and he froze.

'Will I pour?' asked Aising.

'Do, pet,' Una told her. The girl complied.

'Will I bring menus?'

'Do, pet,' repeated Una, leaving no one in any doubt as to who was in charge.

Within seconds, Aising was back with four menus. She handed them out and Una dismissed her.

'We'll give you a shout when we're ready to order.' The minute she'd gone, Una began proceedings. 'Now then,' she told Terrence, 'the first thing on the agenda is for you to drink that whiskey. You're going to need it.' The priest didn't ask questions, he knocked it back in one.

Una reached into her bag for the yellow rubber gloves and put them on. Then she pulled out two clear plastic bags and laid them on the table. She slid them across to Inspector Quinn.

'Be careful,' she told him. 'Don't touch the contents. I'm relying on you to pay for lunch so I'd like you to live through it.'

'It's you who'll be paying for mine if you've got me here on a wild goose chase,' he replied. 'You still haven't told me who the alleged murder victims are.'

Una picked up one of the plastic bags and pulled out the disc. 'I did tell you I had the murder weapon though,' she said, holding it aloft. 'We removed it from Lady Geraldine's slipper.'

'Lady Geraldine? Do you mean Lady Geraldine Hennessy of Moonbeg Manor?'

'That's right.'

'I heard she'd died suddenly, but there's been no mention of a murder.'

'That's because no one knows she was murdered except for those of us sitting around this table, and of course whoever killed her.'

He peered at the disc Una was still holding aloft. 'And you say that's the murder weapon? What is it?'

'Poison,' declared Una. 'It's fiendish but simple. Two plastic discs have been glued together around the edge to form a little bladder, and if you look closely there's a tiny hypodermic needle attached to the centre of the top disc. It was sewn into one of the insoles of a pair of slippers sent to Lady Geraldine for her birthday the day she died. As soon as she put them on, the poison was administered through the sole of her foot.'

'Where did you find the slippers?'

'The cook had thrown them into Lelia's wardrobe but when we looked for them, they'd gone. We found them hidden in the woods.'

'Who's Lelia?'

'The housekeeper.'

'I'll need to question her.'

'That might prove difficult. She's dead too.'

'So the housekeeper is the second murder victim? When did she die?'

'The day after her mistress.' The Inspector looked at the second plastic bag.

'And is that what killed her?'

'No. It's my opinion that Lelia found Lady Geraldine dead and took advantage of the opportunity. I think she stole some things from her room, including the new slippers, and left the body to be discovered by someone else. We found some of her employer's jewellery hidden in her room. When she put the slippers on, though, she got more than she bargained for.'

Una slipped the first disc back inside its bag and carefully removed the other. 'This one was intended for the Monsignor here. We found it in the tack room, inside his riding saddle.'

Gerard was having a hard time taking in all this information, let alone believing any of it. He scratched his head as Una slipped the second disc back inside its bag.

'So you see, Inspector, Joan and I have already done the donkey work for you. There's just one more item on the agenda.'

'Go on,' he sighed, 'nothing would surprise me now.'

'We have to fake the Monsignor's death. Whoever planted the poison in his saddle clearly wants him dead. We have to make them think their murder attempt has been successful.'

Gerard glanced at Terrence who had been sitting quietly up until now. The priest took a long pull from his Guinness.

'Don't look at me,' he said. 'Nobody bothered asking if I agree to any of this.'

'That's because you don't have a choice,' replied Una. 'You're going out riding tomorrow.'

'I'd like to know what happens when my mother hears of my demise.'

'I'm sending you to stay with your mother. We have to hide you somewhere so you'll go to Kinsale for a while.'

'That's not going to happen,' he told her. 'I can barely tolerate my mother in small doses and the feeling is mutual. I'm not staying in the same house as her for any length of time.'

'Stop being difficult, it won't be for long. Now here's what's going to happen. You'll give Matty and Frances the day off tomorrow. At two in the afternoon, you'll start out on your ride.' She turned to Gerard. 'At three o'clock, Inspector, you will have arranged for a couple of police cars to turn up at Moonbeg. They'll cordon off the entrance to the estate and soon after that, an ambulance will come to pick up the body. From that point on, Monsignor McCarthy will be officially dead. You can organise the logistics, can't you Inspector?'

'Well yes, but....'

'Good, then that's agreed.'

Terrence didn't look at all happy, but it wasn't his impending death that worried him.

'Mrs. Murphy, would you mind if I stayed with you instead of with my mother?'

'Well of course, if you'd rather.'

'At the risk of asking a silly question,' said Gerard, 'is it absolutely necessary to fake the Monsignor's death in order to expose the murderer?'

'Let me put it this way, Inspector Quinn. You can either go through a lengthy extradition process to bring the guilty to justice or you can let me hand-deliver them.'

'So you know who it is?'

'O'course I know who it is.'

'You seem to know a lot, Mrs. Murphy. I wonder if you know that withholding information on a crime is a crime in itself?'

'Arrest me so.' She offered the Inspector her wrists, inviting him to handcuff her. 'But I'm warning you, if you do you'll never catch the murderers.'

'Murderers? You mean there's more than one?'

'That's precisely what I mean.'

W.A. Patterson

CHAPTER 18

Terrence hadn't eaten breakfast and now his stomach rumbled like distant thunder. He pressed his hands to it in an attempt to muffle the sound.

'Are you hungry?' asked Una.

'Hungry? I could eat the balls off a low-flying duck.'

'Monsignor!' Joan was outraged. 'What kind of talk is that for a distinguished member of the clergy?'

'He's from Cork,' Una told Gerard apologetically, as if that in itself explained the priest's occasional lapses in decorum. The Inspector nodded sagely. Apparently it did.

'And what's wrong with being from Cork?' Terrence felt suddenly protective of his native county.

'Only good thing ever to come out of Cork was the M8,' quipped Gerard, with a wry grin. Terrence glared at him.

'The road to Tipperary,' explained the Inspector. 'I was on it today.'

'I know what the M8 is!'

The rivalry between counties Cork and Tipperary was legendary, with each generation passing down its ancient and innate sense of tribal superiority to the next. Una felt as if she was back in the school playground.

'Lads, lads, behave yourselves! We're all on the same side here. Terrence, decide what you want to eat. The Inspector's buying.'

'I'm perfectly capable of buying my own lunch,' mumbled the priest sulkily.

Aisling came to take their order and they began discussing the menu, all except for Terrence. His home county had been slighted and he wasn't going to let it pass.

Joan opted for a Chicken Caesar Salad while Una chose Bacon and Cabbage. Gerard ordered the Bacon Cheeseburger. Judging by the amount of Americans who ate here, he assumed the chef must have perfected the dish by now. Terrence glowered at the menu, his expression one of a sullen teenager.

'Smoked salmon terrine,' he said, finally, 'followed by sirloin steak.' He handed the menu back to the blonde. 'Medium rare,' he added, shooting Gerard a smug smile. The Inspector remained pan-faced but when Aisling came to collect his menu, he whispered something to her.

They ate their meals in relative silence, punctuated only by occasional small talk. When they'd finished and the plates had been cleared away, Aisling presented Gerard with a wallet containing the bill. When she presented Terrence with a second wallet, he tried not to show his dismay. After all, he still had an ace up his sleeve. It was his turn to whisper to the waitress.

'O'course, Monsignor,' she replied. A moment later she reappeared and took away both bills. 'Mr. McCarthy says it's on the house, Father. He asked if you'd kindly remember him at Mass on Sunday.'

Terrence grinned. 'That's very kind, tell him I will of course.' Aisling disappeared, leaving Una open-mouthed.

'What's going on?'

'I got her to tell him I spent all my cash here last night. I said I'd pay him next time, but it seems that won't be necessary.'

Gerard shook his head, but he had to smile. 'Well, thanks for the meal.'

'My pleasure, Inspector. Free meals are one of the perks that come with the collar.' There was an aura of smug satisfaction in the priest's demeanor that Una didn't like but she put it aside. She went over the plan once more and, when she was satisfied that everyone was on board, she called the waitress back.

'Give me a menu, would you pet? I'd like to take one home.'

'Are you planning on coming back?' asked Gerard.

'I might, but that's not why I want the menu. I have other plans for it.'

'A cryptic answer as usual, Mrs. Murphy.'

'Sure cryptic is my second language, Inspector.'

On the way out, Una stopped to peruse an assortment of flyers, advertisements and business cards that were pinned to a wall just inside the door.

'Looking for something in particular?' asked the priest. 'There's a lonely hearts section here. How about this one? Wealthy attractive man, 79, seeks strict retired school teacher. Must have own cane.'

'Where?'

'Ha! Got ya!'

Una clipped the priest's ear. Gerard couldn't help but smile at the joke. He'd never seen anyone get the better of Una Murphy before.

Once outside, the Inspector called for a patrol car to pick him up. The others declined his offer of a lift back to Moonbeg but, while Joan and Terrence began walking slowly back towards the priest's car, Una had a quick word with him. She caught them up just as they were passing a small newsagent and she ducked inside. She came out holding a small brown paper bag.

'What's that,' asked the priest.

'Super glue.'

'What do you need it for?'

'To glue your lips together so you'll stop asking questions,' she replied, sarcastically. 'And while we're on the subject of keeping our mouths shut, you're not to tell a soul about our plans. No one else is to know and that includes Matty, do you understand?'

'I feel bad about deceiving poor Matty. He'll be devastated when he thinks I'm dead.'

'I know and I'm sorry, but we can't afford to risk him running his mouth off in the pub after a skinful. If our scheme goes awry, the next attempt on your life could well be successful.' The lighthearted banter of the pub was a world away now and the conversation had taken a darker turn.

'I understand,' said Terrence solemnly, 'I won't say a word.'

'Good, now why don't we take a little stroll to digest our lunch. You can show us around Fethard.'

'Are you sure, my dear? asked Joan. 'What about your poor hip?'

'Ah feck the hip. If it starts acting up I'll find somewhere to sit down. I'm not going to let a gammy hip rule me life.'

Terrence turned out to be an excellent tour guide. He showed the two friends around the Medieval town with its 14th-century walls and monastic ruins, and he related the local folklore. He told them about a local man by the name of John 'Red' Kelly who stole two pigs in 1840 and was shipped to Australia for his crime. He said Red's son Ned had done well too. He'd gone on to rob the landed gentry and become Australia's most notorious outlaw.

Terrence had parked his car at the parochial house. Next to it stood a 12th-century Augustinian Abbey and, when they arrived, he showed them around it. There was a Sheela na Gig carved into the stone above the door, one of many such architectural grotesques found on ancient churches. They depicted naked women with exaggerated private parts, but Una noticed that this one was different to most. She was painfully thin and her ribs stuck out. Her eyes were vacant and staring and her boney arms reached down to her genitalia. Joan was repulsed by the carving but Una was enthralled by the symbolism.

On the journey home Una sat in the front with Terrence and, much to Joan's dismay, their conversation centred around Sheela na Gigs. The prim Englishwoman was aware of their historical significance but, if she had her way, they would all be chiselled from the walls. Una was fascinated by the dichotomy of the one in Fethard. She'd seen others but they were usually corpulent figures. After all, they represented fertility and so, by definition, were portrayed as being well fed. The Fethard one seemed to combine fertility with emaciation and Una put forward her theory that perhaps it was meant to symbolise both life and death in a single persona.

Finally, Joan had heard enough. 'If you persist in discussing that revolting thing,' she exclaimed, 'you can let me out. I'll walk back.'

Una grinned and Terrence chuckled. 'Apologies, Mrs. Cahill,' he said. 'You decide on the topic of conversation.'

'Well for a start, I'd like to know how you intend explaining your impending death to your superiors.'

Una and the priest grew silent. 'I hadn't thought of that,' he said.

'Me neither,' added Una. 'Fair play, Joan, it's a good point. We'd better put on our thinking caps and come up with something, otherwise poor Terrence here might be shipped off to Australia like Red Kelly when the powers that be find out.'

'I've always found honesty to be the best policy,' offered Joan. 'It's my belief that one should take the high road, even if it's not always the easiest route.'

'That's very commendable, pet,' replied Una, 'but in my experience honesty isn't always the best policy. Sometimes taking the high road can lead you straight off a cliff.'

CHAPTER 19

By the time they arrived back at Moonbeg Manor it was late afternoon. The day was still warm and sunny so they ordered tea and sat chatting in a shady corner of the walled garden.

'I think Joan's right,' mused Terrence. 'I don't think we have any choice other than for me to come clean.'

Finn had been ecstatic with joy when his mistress first arrived back. He liked the big house with its expansive playground and he loved the tall friend he'd made in Matty but Una was his world and, like all dogs when their owners leave the house, he was never really sure if she'd ever come back. Within minutes of her arrival, however, he was back to his bold, cocky self. He abandoned her to sniff the priest's trouser legs and became so obsessed with them that

Terrence had to bat him away. The little terrier was now busy digging up an herbaceous border.

'Let's not be too hasty,' said Una. 'There's always room for a little creativity when it comes to the truth. Finn! Spit that out!' The little dog took up a defiant stance and wagged his tail. He had something in his mouth again.

'It's alright for you,' replied the priest. 'It's not you they might exile to a remote parish in the back end of beyond. What's that dog got now?'

'It's a worm, and don't try and pull the wool over my eyes, Monsignor McCarthy. I know how much power you wield in Church circles, and outside them. You got poor Kitty Egan's body removed from the mortuary easily enough.'

'Kitty Egan? Ah yes, well someone higher up the food chain handled that. I didn't have very much at all to do with it. That dog of yours really does have some disgusting habits.'

Joan had been listening to their exchange. 'May I offer a solution?' she said.

'Give the scruffy mutt away?' he grinned. Una glared at him.

'I meant a solution to our other problem,' giggled Joan.

'By all means.'

'You have a law degree, Monsignor, am I right?'

'That is correct.'

'And I assume that you specialise in ecclesiastical law.'

'Right again.'

'You said the Kitty Egan case was handled by other Church officials. Who authorised it?'

'Even if I knew the answer to that, I wouldn't be able to tell you.'

'I know all about lawyer-client privilege, my late husband was a solicitor, but what would happen if the details of the bog body case were to become public?'

'I don't understand. That's all in the past. What relevance does it have to our situation?'

'Una entered into a confidentiality agreement with you back then and, by association, with the Church. Isn't that the case?

'I suppose so.'

'Well I know as much about the case as Una and I didn't agree to keep it to myself, did I?'

'Well no, but......'

'So what's stopping me from going public with the Church's involvement in Kitty's death and the cover-up years later? The threat of that happening must surely be enough to keep your superiors quiet.'

'I think you'll find that's blackmail, Mrs. Cahill.'

'Blackmail is such an ugly word,' replied Joan airily. 'I prefer leverage.'

'And that would make me a participant after the fact. I could be disbarred.'

'Oh I doubt it would come to that. A suspension, a fine perhaps, and that's only if your involvement came to light. After all, you weren't aware of how much I knew at the time.'

Terrence mulled it over in his mind for a few minutes. Finally, he set his mouth in a decisive thin line and pulled a mobile phone out of his pocket.

'I have Archbishop Loughlin's number,' he said. 'Let's get this over with.' He took a gulp of lukewarm tea and scowled at the cup as if it was somehow at fault for cooling its own contents. He got up from the table and wandered off in the direction of the house, mumbling to himself as if rehearsing lines. Una watched as he walked away.

'Curious,' she mumbled

'What's curious, dear?'

'Ah don't mind me, pet.' Una rubbed her hip. 'Agh! I hate getting old.'

'Well I did say you should have taken the walking stick.'

'And as much as it grieves me to say it, on this occasion you were right. This tea is cold,' she complained, absently waving away a bumblebee that hovered over her cup.

The priest returned after twenty minutes.

'Did you have to use my leverage option?' asked Joan.

'No, I thought of something else,' he said, flapping his hand dismissively. 'So anyway, now that I can give the case my undivided attention, Mrs. Murphy, are you prepared to tell me who it is we're hoping to bring to justice?'

Una smiled inscrutably. 'Not quite yet, Monsignor.' She turned to Joan. 'Could I borrow that little pair of scissors from your manicure set again, pet?'

*

They returned to the house and Terrence went to sit in the drawing room. Joan headed straight upstairs, while Una took a detour to the kitchen. She'd run out of treats for Finn so she procured a carrot from

Frances. Finn enjoyed the odd raw carrot, though he rarely got them at home because of the mess he made eating them. Una had work to do and she didn't have time to entertain her hyperactive dog. She knew from experience that the rock-hard root vegetable would keep him occupied for half an hour at least.

When she got to her room, Joan was already waiting with the manicure set, as requested. Una emptied out the contents of her own handbag onto the bed. She picked up the menu she'd brought from McCarthys and pulled it out of its clear plastic sleeve. Then she took a two euro coin from her purse. It was the largest of the Irish coins and would serve her purpose well. She placed it onto the plastic wallet, then traced around the edge of it with a pen. Joan watched with interest.

'What are you doing, dear?'

'I'm making one of those little bladder yokes.'

'Like the one used to poison Geraldine?'

'And the one planted inside Terrence's saddle, yes.'

'But why?'

'Because we took the deadly one out of the saddle. I'm making a replacement.'

'You don't have a hypodermic needle.'

'No, but I've got this.' Una rummaged through the items she'd tossed out of her bag and held up a drawing pin. She had surreptitiously removed it from the wall inside McCarthys door, where all the ads and flyers were displayed.

'That? It doesn't look anything like a needle.'

'Not yet. It will by the time I'm finished with it… hopefully, anyway.'

Finn was busy gnawing his way through the carrot, making a terrible mess on the bedroom carpet in the process. Joan clucked her tongue.

'There's something very odd about a dog who eats carrots,' she sniffed.

'What do the royal corgis eat? Caviar?'

'Actually, they have fresh meat prepared by the Queen's chefs. The only vegetable they're given is cabbage and that's only so they don't get.... well, bunged up.'

Una was still busy working on her project. 'Don't tell me you actually know what the Queen's dogs have for dinner. You'll be telling me next they have their own little doggie menu.'

'As a matter of fact, they do.'

'Jayzus, now I've heard it all. Give me those nail clippers, would you?'

Una began nipping away at the plastic thumb tack on the end of the drawing pin. After a few minutes it cracked and she was left with what looked like a little brad nail. She held it up for Joan to see.

'It still looks nothing like a hypodermic, dear. It just looks like a small nail, and it's far too long.'

'I'm not finished yet!' retorted Una. Using the nail clippers, she tried to cut it to a more appropriate length, but it was harder than she'd anticipated. Finally she used both hands and with an almighty effort, squeezed as hard as she could. There was a resounding ping as the metal gave way.

'There!' she said triumphantly.

'You broke my clippers!'

'Never mind your clippers, I'll get you a new pair.'

'But I've had those over twenty years.'

'Well it's about time you had some new ones so.'

'You're not going to break anything else, are you?'

'I'm going to break open that super glue if I can find it.'

Joan retrieved the little tube of glue from the contents of Una's bag and deftly broke off the cap, anxious that her friend might drip the contents onto the expensive counterpane. Five minutes and several glued-together fingers later, Una held up the finished article for inspection.

'Oh yes, that's more like it,' agreed Joan, 'but I still don't understand why we have to replace the one we took from the saddle. Why bother?'

'It's important that we put everything back the way we found it. We can't chance anyone seeing us though. I'll get Matty to take Finn for a walk in the woods. That should give us time to do it without being seen.'

'Are we involving Terrence in this?'

'No, he doesn't need to know. In fact it's better if he doesn't.'

'So what's the plan after his supposed death tomorrow?'

'Well we've set the mousetrap but we still have to put the cheese in it. We can do that from home though. We'll get Gerard to take us back to Ballyanny tomorrow morning.'

Joan shuddered. 'All this talk of death is most disturbing, I won't be at all sorry when this case is over.'

'Ah but the best is yet to come, pet!'

Finn had just about demolished his carrot now and the unexpected intake of fibre had given him a severe bout of flatulence. He made his way purposefully towards Joan and the foul-smelling gas followed him like a noxious cloud. When the fetid odour reached her nose, she squeezed her nostrils together with one hand and flapped the other wildly in front of her face.

'I sometimes wonder which is more infuriating,' she exclaimed, her tone nasal, 'you or that disgusting animal of yours. Ugh!'

CHAPTER 20

It was half three in the afternoon by the time Matty finally made it into work. He looked very much the worse for wear after his heavy drinking session the night before and, when Una asked him to take Finn for a walk in the woods, he gladly obliged. He wasn't sure if his sore head would survive the sound of noisy power tools today. As soon as they'd disappeared out of sight, the two friends made their way to the barn. Una carefully inserted her decoy device inside the saddle and glued the leather neatly back in place.

'How's that, Joan? Does it look as if it's been tampered with?'

'Not at all. You've done an excellent job.'

'Grand, let's make ourselves scarce so. We'll go back inside and act the innocent.'

'We're old women, dear. People automatically assume we're innocent.'

'And it is precisely for that reason, my deah,' replied Una, with an exaggerated English accent, 'that we are so frightfully dangerous.'

'You're getting rather good at imitating me,' said Joan, her tongue firmly planted in her cheek. 'We'll make an Englishwoman of you yet.' Una's mimicry had backfired on her and she put her hands on her ample hips.

'There's nothing English about me, Joan Cahill, I'm pure Irish and proud of it! It took us eight hundred years to get rid of you lot and if you think I want to....'

'Your English counterparts didn't have it easy either,' interrupted Joan. 'The poor were mistreated in England too, especially if they were Catholic. It was only the Protestant upper classes who thrived.'

'Well you'd know all about the snobby upper classes!'

'Are we going to stand here and argue all day, or shall we go and get a cup of tea before one of us says something we might regret?'

'Ah you're right, pet. Baiting the trap is the most important thing now.' They began making their way back towards the house.

'And I'll have you know,' said Joan, 'I'm not upper class. Your background's similar to mine.'

'It is in me hole! My Da was a blacksmith; yours was Master of the Hunt!'

'Well horses need shoes, don't they? Blacksmiths make horseshoes. My father was on very good terms with our farrier.'

'*Our farrier*, sez Her Ladyship! I rest my case.'

The conversation continued in a similar vein all the way to the kitchen but, by the time the two friends were seated at the table, its subject matter had been forgotten. It was a common occurrence, one of the few silver linings that accompanied the cloud of old age. No doubt the same verbal exchange would be repeated at a later date, quite possibly on more than one occasion.

Frances poured their tea, then busied herself preparing dinner. Una stirred hers vigorously, tinkling her spoon loudly against the sides of the china cup. She glanced over at Frances, then leaned in towards Joan.

'It's Johann, by the way,' she said in a low voice.

'What is, dear?'

'The murderer, of course, it's Johann.' Una had raised her voice slightly and although

Frances didn't turn around, she stopped peeling the potatoes.

'But how do you know?' Joan was startled by her friend's sudden revelation.

'He has the means for a start, he's a toxicologist. He has motive too, the inheritance. I'm afraid there's absolutely no doubt, Johann is the murderer.'

'Good lord, how awful.'

'By the way, pet, we have to make an early start tomorrow. After Terrence has driven us home, he wants to come back here to do a little riding before he heads down to Kinsale to visit his mother.'

Frances resumed peeling, her back still to the table, and Joan jutted her chin in the cook's direction. Una smiled and nodded, then sipped her tea. The two friends sat in silence until the last drop of tea had been drained from their cups.

'Well, I'm going up to pack, dear,' said Joan.

'Good idea, pet, our work here is done.' They left the kitchen together and climbed the stairs. At the top, Joan grabbed Una's arm.

'Did you see that?' she said, in a hoarse whisper. 'Frances was listening to every word you said.'

'Thank the Lord. I thought I was going to have to throw my spoon at her to get her attention.'

'What do you mean?'

'A little bit of the cheese, pet,' replied Una, heading for her bedroom with Joan following close behind.

'Must you always speak in riddles?'

'You nibbled a bit of it and unless I'm very much mistaken, so did Frances.'

'You do realise she won't keep what she heard to herself.'

'I'm counting on it.'

'Oh I see. You're laying a false trail, is that it?'

'Did you ever hear the tale of Galloping Hogan?'

'There you go again. Why can't you just give a simple answer to a simple question? Why does it always have to be cryptic or accompanied by some story or other?'

'Ah but you'll like this one, pet, it has to do with horseshoes.'

'Why would I like a story about horseshoes?'

'Weren't we talking about them earlier?'

'Were we? I can't remember. Anyway, who's this Hurrying Hogan fellow?'

'I said Galloping Hogan, cloth ears! He was an infamous highwayman and the story goes that he nailed the shoes onto his horse backwards. That way, the sheriff who followed his tracks went in the wrong direction. Isn't that genius?'

'So what you're saying is that Johann isn't the murderer at all.'

'Of course not. Johann is the vice-president of a multi-national pharmaceutical company. He has enough money in salary and stocks to buy ten of these estates.'

'How do you know that?'

'I googled him last night.'

'And you didn't think of sharing this with me?'

'I probably should have, pet, but the truth is I'm not exactly certain who committed the murders now. There are definitely two people involved and I had thought one of them was Johann. I believe I know who the other is but, if I'm not very much mistaken, we'll find out for sure when the Monsignor's death is announced. If my plan works, the murderers should give themselves away.'

They were in Una's bedroom by now and Finn scampered in, wringing wet. Una was surprised, it was dry and sunny outside. The undergrowth carpeting the floor of the woods must be damper than she thought. The little terrier went to stand beside Joan before shaking himself off.

'Oh for goodness' sake!' she shrieked, backing away from the dense mist of water droplets. 'That vile animal of yours!'

'He only goes to you because he likes you.'

'Because he hates me, you mean.' Joan tried to flick off the beads of water that had landed on her clothes before they soaked in. In the meantime, Finn had moved in on her and now he shook himself again.

'See? He's doing it on purpose!' The little dog sat down and looked at Joan, his head cocked sideways, an angelic expression on his face. 'Look!' she exclaimed. 'He's mocking me again!'

'Not at all, sure he adores the upper classes. That's his subservient face.'

'Well he's not fooling me, and don't think I didn't catch that little dig of yours. I'm going back to my room before you start blaming me personally for your eight hundred years of oppression.' Joan wheeled round and stalked out of the room, mumbling something about old grudges.

Una soon had her packing done and she went downstairs with Finn at her heels. As it was their last evening, they were to eat in the formal dining room and when she got there, Terrence and Matty had already taken their places at the table. Matty had a linen serviette tucked inside his collar like a bib and was holding his knife and fork in his big hands, even though there was no food on the table as yet. Joan arrived a few minutes later. The only place setting left available was opposite Matty and she took it reluctantly.

'Did you and Finn enjoy your walk, Matty?' asked Una.

'We did, missus, but the little fella rolled in a pile o' cow shit. I had to wash him down.' That explained why Finn had come in soaking wet.

'Really!' gasped Joan. 'That kind of talk is simply unacceptable at the dinner table!'

'Sorry missus, I don't know how else to say it.'

'Then don't say anything at all.'

'But Mrs. Murphy asked me a question.' The big fellow was confused and looked to Terrence for help. The priest just shook his head and smiled. Luckily, Frances came in carrying an enormous silver platter containing a huge joint of roast beef. Half the meat was already carved and the joint was encircled with floury potatoes in their jackets. When she put the platter on the table Matty's eyes lit up, his hurt feelings already a dim memory.

'Ah Frances, me oul' segotia,' he grinned, 'you know the way to a man's heart alright.

Will ya ever marry me before someone else snaps me up?'

He slapped her buttock as she turned to walk away and she clipped him around the ear. Joan's nerves had begun to unravel like the strings of an old fiddle and they were dangerously near the point of snapping.

Matty piled his plate high with food until it looked as though half of it might tumble off onto the table at any moment.

'Why don't you simply go back for seconds?' asked Joan, exasperated by his loutish table manners.

'T'anks, missus, I will, but I have to eat this first.'

Terrence and Una glanced at each other and tried not to smile. They all watched as Matty reached for a pepper pot. He turned it upside down and the lid fell off, sending a deluge of white pepper cascading down onto his food. Terrence suppressed a laugh, he knew this must be sheer torture for Mrs. Cahill.

Matty stared at the mound of dusty condiment for a moment, then shrugged his shoulders and began mixing it into his potatoes. Some pepper had found its way into his nostrils and he closed his eyes as he tilted back his head. He opened his mouth and inhaled, but before he had a chance to follow through, Joan slid back her chair and got up from the table. Sitting opposite, she had no desire to be in his firing line.

They all braced themselves and when the big man finally did sneeze, it was so violent that the table shook. He blew his nose loudly on the linen napkin draped around his neck and that was the last straw for Joan. The camel's back had been broken and so had her nerves. She excused herself, saying she'd suddenly lost her appetite and was going for a lie down. Matty was already shovelling food into his mouth and didn't even notice the Englishwoman had left the room.

Una and Terrence helped themselves from the various serving dishes that Frances had brought in and, apart from the sound of Matty chomping on his food, the main course passed in relative silence. Frances wasn't eating with them that evening and when they had finished, she came in and cleared away the plates.

'I've a lovely bread and butter pudding for afters,' she told them, 'I'll bring it in.' She left the room, but the sight of her seemed to jog something in Matty's memory.

'Agh, the bastard!' he snarled.

'Who's a bastard?' said Terrence, startled by the big man's outburst.

'Johann. If I could get me hands on him, I'd put me fist right through his face!'

Terrence looked at Una in bewilderment. She smiled to herself. Another bit of cheese had been nibbled. At this rate there would soon be none left and nothing to stop the trap's spring from being triggered. The jaws would snap shut and whoever committed the murders would be trapped firmly between them.

CHAPTER 21

Frances set down a large dish of bread and butter pudding on the table.

'Why don't you join us?' said Terrence. 'There's plenty to go round now Mrs. Cahill isn't here.'

'I don't mind if I do, Father. Thank you.'

Frances took Joan's place at the table and spooned herself out a serving before passing the dish. Una spooned a tiny portion of the pudding into her dessert bowl.

'Not that fond of bread and butter pudding, missus?' asked Frances.

'Ah, I have a dirty liking for it.'

'I haven't heard that expression in donkey's years,' laughed Terrence. 'I'm not a fan of anything with dried fruit in it.'

'I've made this for you before, Father,' said Frances. 'You ate it then.'

'I didn't want to seem ungrateful, Frances. My father used to tell me the raisins were dead flies. It put me off bread and butter pudding for life.' He reached for a large jug that Frances had brought in with the pudding. 'Custard, now that's a different matter.' He poured himself a generous helping and handed the jug to Una. She drowned her small portion of pudding in the creamy vanilla sauce. Matty had been looking on in anticipation.

'Everyone done?'

They all nodded and he reached for the pudding dish. He poured what remained of the warm, yellow custard into it and tucked in. Una was relieved that Joan wasn't there to witness the spectacle.

'By the way, Matty,' said Terrence, 'you can have tomorrow off. I'm taking Mrs. Murphy and Mrs. Cahill back to Ballyanny and I won't be needing you.' Matty pinched his eyes shut and swallowed a large bolus of half-masticated pudding.

'But I thought you was coming back here to ride.' A little more of the cheese had been nibbled.

'I might, I might not, depends on how I feel. Anyway, I can manage without you.'

'It's forecast fine anyway,' said Matty, 'should be a lovely day fer a ride. A grand day fer drivin' down to Cork after too.'

'Well yes, I.... Wait a minute. How did you know I was planning on driving to Cork? I didn't tell you.' Frances stopped eating but she didn't take her eyes off her dish. Matty shrugged.

'Dunno. Must o' heard it somewhere.' The cook tried to kick him under the table but she missed and clipped the priest's shin.

'Ouch! What was that for?'

'Sorry, Father, me foot slipped.' It was time for Una to divert the conversation before Terrence thwarted their plans. She cleared her throat and adopted an officious tone.

'I'd like to thank you, Monsignor, on behalf of Joan and myself, for a wonderful few days. We have enjoyed our time at Moonbeg Manor immensely.'

'Think nothing of it,' replied Terrence, rubbing his shin and glaring at Frances. Matty had the last of the bread and butter pudding in his mouth now and said something incoherent. Terrence's mood was as sore as his leg.

'Swallow your bloody food before you speak, man!' he snapped.

The big fellow gulped mightily and repeated his statement. 'I said there's horse liniment in the barn if yer leg's sore.'

'Thanks, but I'd rather not smell like a cough drop for the rest of the day. I'll walk it off.' Frances began clearing the table. She avoided the priest's glare. 'We'll take our tea in the garden,' he told her.

'Of course, sir,' she mumbled, hurrying out of the room with a large tray of dishes. Matty lumbered out behind her, hands in pockets.

'Good idea,' said Una. 'We should just catch the late afternoon sun. Have you seen Finn, by the way?'

'Not for a while. He's probably destroying something priceless.'

'*Finn*!' yelled Una, startling the priest. '*Walk*!' Within seconds, the dog scampered into the dining room, a remnant of carpet fabric in his mouth. 'Oh dear,' she said, 'these rugs aren't Persian, are they?'

'Of course they're Persian! Aunt Geraldine would have nothing less. Jesus, that dog has done more damage to this house than the IRA did during the Civil War!'

'Ah stop complaining. When you hear what I have to tell you, you'll be kissing Finn's arse.'

'Believe me, Mrs. Murphy, nothing would entice me to put my lips anywhere near that dog's rear end.'

'Ah, but you haven't heard what he did yet.'

They made their way outside into the walled garden. It was already eight o'clock but the evening was still balmy. They made themselves comfortable on the wooden chairs and Una closed her eyes as she offered up her face to the warm sun.

'So what exactly has that animal of yours done,' said Terrence, interrupting Una's reverie, 'apart from systematically destroy the contents of Moonbeg Manor?'

'Let me alone for a minute, I'm enjoying the sunshine.'

The priest realised he would nothing out of the old woman until she was good and ready, so he too sat back and soaked up the sun. The combination of its warmth and a full stomach soon had him seduced into the netherworld between consciousness and sleep. He vaguely heard the chatter of women and was weaving it into a nonsensical dream where their voices were coming from out of a dog's hairy backside when Una poked him with her elbow.

'Sorry,' he said, rubbing his eyes. 'I must have dozed off for a minute.'

'More like half an hour,' replied Joan. Terrence was surprised to see that Mrs. Cahill had joined them. She smiled sweetly at him.

'Really? Did I miss anything?' Joan opened her mouth to speak but Una put her hand on her friend's knee.

'Not much,' she said. 'Just two old women blathering on.'

'So about your dog. You said Finn had done something I should be grateful for.'

'That's right,' replied Una. 'He saved your life.'

The priest looked around for the dog and spotted him at the other end of the garden, methodically digging up a line of geranium plants.

'I don't understand, but that's nothing new. I don't understand any of what's going on around here lately. You two ladies seem to get some sort of perverse satisfaction out of keeping me in the dark. Would you care to enlighten me?'

'When Joan and I inspected the barn, we didn't find anything out of place until Finn led us to the tack room. We didn't even know what we were looking for. It was Finn who took us straight to the saddle with the poison in it. He was the one that saved your life.'

'Well, well. Then I am indeed indebted to him.'

'As far as the rest of it's concerned, I'm afraid we have to keep you in the dark a little longer. We need you to behave as you would normally. If we told you our plan, then you wouldn't act natural.'

'You might be surprised. You learn to be a good actor in my line of work.'

'Believe me, Monsignor,' said Una, 'I'm almost old enough to have known William Shakespeare himself and I can tell you, you're no Laurence Olivier.'

CHAPTER 22

The big house seemed eerily quiet when the two friends came down next morning. The usual clatter made by Frances preparing breakfast was conspicuous by its absence, as was Frances herself. They made themselves a pot of tea and took it out into the garden on a tray, along with a packet of plain digestive biscuits they'd found, determined to make the most of their last hours at Moonbeg Manor. Una had given up yelling at Finn so she ignored him as he set about excavating a couple of begonias.

It was a good hour before Terrence finally put in an appearance. He was dressed in a bathrobe and slippers, his mop of curly dark hair damp and uncombed.

'You look like shite,' Una told him. 'Didn't you get any sleep?'

'Not a wink.'

'It's hardly surprising,' said Joan. 'Who could sleep with the knowledge that they're going to die the next day?'

'I'm going to have to call my mother too. I think that prospect was equally responsible for my insomnia. Ringing her isn't something I relish doing.'

'Oh but you must,' urged Joan. 'Imagine if she was to hear it on the news.'

He chuckled. 'The shock might kill the old witch.'

'I fail to see the humour. Regardless of your differences, she is still your mother.'

'She'll want to visit you know, when I'm in Ballyanny I mean, just to make sure I'm not dead.'

'What's wrong with that? Any mother would do the same.'

'You haven't met her,' he mumbled. 'Is that tea still hot? I'm gagging.'

Una handed him the pot. 'No, you'll have to make some more. I wouldn't mind another cup myself.' The priest snatched the teapot out of her hand and marched back towards the house.

Joan leaned towards her friend. 'If his mother is as intimidating as he makes out,' she said, 'I'm not altogether sure I want to meet her.'

'Ah she can't be all that bad, and if she is we'll send her packing. One Irish rebuff is just as effective as a hundred thousand welcomes.'

Joan giggled. 'You're incorrigible, Mrs. Murphy.'

'Thank you, pet.'

Terrence returned with a full, heavy teapot in one hand and a cup in the other. He dumped the pot down roughly on the table.

'Damn and blast it!'

'What on earth's the matter?' asked Una.

'I scalded my hand!'

'Jesus, can't you even make a pot of tea without injuring yourself?'

'Madam! When I want tea, I'm accustomed to having someone serve it to me.'

Una turned to Joan. 'Did he just call me Madam?'

'He did, dear.'

'And did I detect a high and mighty attitude?'

'That's certainly how it came across.'

She glared at the priest until he had to turn away. He picked up the teapot.

'Will I pour yours?' he asked, sheepishly.

'You will not! Unlike you, Monsignor McCarthy, I don't need anyone to pour my tea. I can even wipe my own a....'

'Ahhh, it's such a beautiful morning!' interrupted Joan. 'The forecast says it's going to be dry and sunny all day.'

'Never mind the weather forecast!' Una had been affronted. 'I won't have some arrogant upstart looking down his nose at me, I don't care who he is.'

Terrence realised he'd overstepped the mark and was hanging on by his fingernails.

'Forgive me,' he said. 'It's myself I'm annoyed with, not you. My tone was inexcusable. I don't know what I would have done without you two ladies these last few days, and I don't dare to imagine what might have happened to me if you hadn't come to stay.' Although his apology was effusive, Una couldn't help feeling it lacked sincerity.

'You'd be dead, young man, that's what! Sit down. I'll pour the tea.'

He held out his cup to her and his hand trembled slightly.

'Pull yourself together, man. Drink your tea then go back upstairs and put your grown-up trousers on. We have work to do.' By the time the pot was empty, Una had calmed down and Terrence was more relaxed.

'Off you go,' she told him. 'We need to get back to Ballyanny as soon as possible.

There are still a few issues that need ironing out.'

'Like what?'

'Well someone has to discover your body for a start. Inspector Quinn is to go riding with you.'

'I didn't know he could ride.'

'He probably can't, but he's only acting the part. He'll wait a sufficient amount of time after you've set out, then he'll put in a call to the Emergency Services. They'll come out and pronounce you dead at the scene. You'll be bundled into the ambulance and off you go.'

'What about the paramedics? They'll soon realise they don't have a dead body on their hands.'

'There won't be any paramedics. Gerard has roped in a couple of his detectives; they'll be manning the ambulance.'

'But won't they need a body, you know, to deliver to the morgue?'

'They have one, some poor fella they pulled out of the River Suir a couple of days ago. A suicide apparently. His body will already be in the ambulance when they pick you up.'

'How on earth do you know all this?'

'You weren't the only one awake last night, Monsignor. I was on the phone with the Inspector. The hard work is done, all you have to do is play dead. Now would you please go and get dressed. If that bathrobe of yours gapes open any further, Joan and I will be treated to an unexpected view of the Holy Land!'

*

An hour later, a black Mercedes purred into the little village of Ballyanny and drew up outside Una Murphy's house. Once inside, the two friends made a beeline for the kitchen while Terrence went upstairs to change into his riding attire. Una had just put the kettle on when there was a knock at the front door.

'I'll go,' she said. 'It'll be Gerard.'

She opened the door and grinned. It was the Inspector alright but instead of his usual wrinkled suit and loosely-knotted tie, he was wearing ill-fitting breeches, a pair of black riding boots that had seen better days and an oversized white shirt. She looked him up and down.

'How do I look?' he asked, bashfully.

'You look the dog's bollix!'

'That doesn't sound good.'

'Not good? It doesn't get any better than the dog's bollix! Now come in, I need to discuss a couple of things with you before Terrence comes down.'

'You do look smart, Inspector,' lied Joan, when he came into the kitchen. 'Sit down, I'll pour you a nice cup of tea.'

Una got right down to business. 'Did you make that phone call we talked about?'

'I did. He assured me the lab is at our disposal.'

'Grand, and did you send him the samples?'

'They've gone by express courier to Amsterdam; we should have the results within forty-eight hours. You know I really should have waited for authority before I did any of this. I hope your plan works, otherwise I'm out of a job.'

'Never mind,' said Una, 'you can always join Terrence in the Australian outback.' The two friends giggled.

'You two women do talk nonsense sometimes. This is a series business, you know.'

Before Una could respond, they heard heavy footsteps on the stairs. Terrence entered the kitchen and the two women's jaws dropped in unison. In contrast to the detective's ill-fitting garb, the priest was impeccably dressed. It almost looked as if he'd been sewn into his riding costume.

'Goodness!' gasped Joan. 'How handsome you look, just like Colin Firth in Pride and Prejudice!'

With one arm across his waist, the priest bowed deeply. 'Madam,' he said. 'Mr. Darcy at your service.'

'Sit down,' snapped Una. 'You've got time for one cup of tea and then it's showtime. Now listen, Terrence, we've decided your death will take place in the barn.'

'In the barn? Why?'

'It's safer. It's the only way we can be certain Gerard is the only witness. After you've saddled your horse, you're to go back inside the barn and lie on the floor as if you've fallen there.'

'But I had my death scene all planned out. I rehearsed it last night when I couldn't sleep.'

'Well your melodramatics aren't required now so drink up. You'll be late.'

'Must you talk to me as if I was a child? I might just as well have gone to my mother's.'

Joan was still admiring Terrence's apparel and the figure he cut in it.

'I couldn't throw a bucket of water over you before you go, could I?' she giggled.

'Control yourself, woman!' admonished Una. 'You're supposed to be a respectable widow.'

Joan sipped her tea and smiled. 'I was widowed, dear,' she said, 'not neutered.'

CHAPTER 23

Una sipped her tea and watched the clock. Joan was squeezing lemons. She liked to keep herself busy when she was nervous and had decided to bake a couple of cakes.

'How many cups of tea is that you've had, Una?'

'I don't know, four maybe. I've had to pee four times and it's usually one pee per cup.'

'Clock-watching never makes the time go quicker you know. Quite the reverse in fact.'

Una sighed. 'I know, I just can't concentrate on anything else. I keep thinking of all the things that could go wrong.'

'Now what could possibly go wrong?'

'Where would you like me to start?' Joan extracted an errant pip from the lemon juice.

'I'm usually the one who worries,' she said. 'Nothing ever seems to faze you.'

'Even I have to admit that we're in over our heads on this one, Joanie. We like to think we're a couple of master detectives. The truth is we're just a pair of elderly amateurs flying by the seat of our pants.'

'Well we haven't crashed yet, dear. We're still in the air.'

'That must be why I feel sick.'

'Why don't you come and help me, it'll help take your mind off things. You can grate the rind.'

'Lemon drizzle, is it?'

'Yes, I'm making two. If the Monsignor's mother does comes, I'll give her one as a gift. If she's as much of a battleaxe as he makes out, it might start us off on a better footing.'

'I'm quite looking forward to meeting her actually.'

Joan glanced at Una and caught the unmistakable twinkle of mischief in her friend's eyes.

'Now then, Una, she'll be a guest in your house. One should always make guests feel welcome, regardless of whether or not one likes them.'

'Well one will behave if she does but if she starts looking down her nose at me, one can't promise anything.'

'It sounds to me like you've already made up your mind. Give the poor woman a chance. If I applied the same standards to you, I'd have stopped talking to you years ago.'

'Me? Agh, sure I'm a pure dote.'

'You can be a veritable harridan when you want to be, Una Murphy, and you know it.'

'I do not know it!' retorted Una, 'I'm not even sure what the word means but I shall be looking it up and if it's not nice, I shall find a very long one meaning gobshite!'

Joan had been purposely distracting her friend from thinking about the events playing out at Moonbeg Manor, but she wasn't in the mood for an argument so she changed the subject.

'Terrence and Gerard should be on their way back soon. What shall we give them for dinner?'

'There's mince in the freezer and a jar of Marinara Sauce in the cupboard. I'll make a nice Spag Bol.'

'Is there any garlic bread to go with it?'

'When have I had time to go to the shops for bread? They'll have to do without.'

'I don't really have time to make it.' Joan pondered for a moment, then a flash of inspiration came to her. 'Fusion!' she exclaimed.

'Stop blurting out random words, Joan. Have you suddenly developed Tourette's?'

'No, fusion! Taking food from two cultures and combining them.'

'I think you've lost another marble, pet.'

'We'll have garlic soda bread!' exclaimed Joan, ignoring her friend. 'I don't have to wait for the dough to prove for soda bread so I've got time to make it.'

'Garlic soda bread? Jayzus! Sounds disgusting.'

'No more disgusting than your pigs trotters!'

'You leave me and my pigs trotters alone. I like a nice dish of crubeens, especially when they're battered and fried.'

'Well I'm going to make garlic soda bread. You don't have to eat it if you don't want to.'

Joan poked holes in her two cakes and drizzled over a mixture of lemon juice and granulated sugar.

'That's them finished,' she said, wiping her hands on a kitchen towel. 'I'm going back home now to make the bread. I wouldn't want to offend your delicate nostrils by filling your kitchen with the smell of garlic.'

'Please yourself.'

*

Half an hour later the two men arrived back and Una immediately sensed tension between them.

'What's the matter,' she said. 'What's happened?'

'Ask him,' replied Gerard, tersely. 'I'm going outside for a smoke.'

'I didn't know you smoked, Inspector.'

'I don't.' He removed an unopened pack of cigarettes from the inside pocket of his coat. 'I gave it up two years ago, kept these on me ever since.' He stormed out of the kitchen, slamming the back door behind him. Una swung round to face Terrence.

'What have you done to annoy him?'

'Me? I didn't do anything.' She folded her arms and glared at him. 'Don't you start!' he told her. 'I've had enough of him treating me like a child.'

'I've never met anyone more even-tempered than Gerard Quinn. Something must have riled him.'

'Look, all I did was give out to him for taking my car away. What am I expected to do? Sit around this God-forsaken place with the rest of the culchies? And if that wasn't enough, he confiscated my mobile phone too!'

Una took the priest by the arm and dragged him over to the kitchen window.

'See that man out there?' she said. 'The one inhaling cigarette smoke like it's going out of fashion? Well he put his job on the line for you today, a complete stranger, and you reward him by acting like a spoiled brat.'

Reluctantly, Terrence looked outside. Gerard was pacing up and down the garden path, stopping only to light one cigarette from another.

'I suppose you're right,' he said, unconvincingly. 'I probably owe him an apology.'

Una swung open the back door and, once the priest was outside, slammed it shut behind him. She couldn't hear their conversation but she could see them through the window.

Terrence spoke first, his head bent, then Gerard looked to be reading him the riot act, using his lit cigarette to emphasise each bullet point. Terrence glanced up a couple of times to make eye contact, otherwise he kept his head bent low. It was a scene that Una had witnessed more times than she cared to remember throughout her teaching career. When the Inspector was satisfied that Terrence was suitably penitent, he offered him his hand and the priest shook it. Gerard dropped his cigarette butt on the path and ground it in with his foot. The two men returned to the house.

Gerard seated himself at the table. 'A cup of tea would be nice if it's not too much trouble, Mrs. Murphy,' he said, 'and one for yer man here.'

'Two teas coming up,' replied Una.

'You wouldn't happen to have a couple of paracetamol, would you?'

'Have you a headache, Gerard?'

'A fierce one.' He closed his eyes and rubbed his temples.

'I suppose that's my fault too,' mumbled Terrence.

'It's what I get for smoking two-year-old cigarettes. I'm as dizzy as a drunk and my head's pounding.'

'I've apologised, haven't I? What more do you want?'

Gerard didn't answer, he just shook his head and blew on his tea. When it had cooled sufficiently, he gulped down two caplets that Una had given him.

'I take it you won't be sending each other Facebook friend requests,' she said.

Gerard chuckled, then winced in pain. 'Don't make me laugh,' he groaned, 'it hurts.'

*

When Joan returned, she was carrying a plate covered with a clean linen tea towel. Gerard inhaled.

'I don't believe it,' he exclaimed. 'That's garlic soda bread, isn't it?'

'Indeed it is,' replied Joan, removing the towel with a flourish.

'Brilliant! I haven't had that in years.'

Una's face contorted in surprise. 'You mean there really is such a thing?' Joan smiled smugly. 'You knew about garlic soda bread all the time, didn't you Joan Cahill.'

'I know a lot of things, Una Murphy.'

The pungent aroma was permeating the room now.

'Ahhhh, reminds me of when I was a kid,' said Gerard, smiling. 'Every spring when the daffodils came up, Mammy would collect leaves from the wild garlic and bake them into her soda bread.'

'Well the leaves are too tough at the moment,' Joan told him. 'I crushed a couple of garlic cloves and some green onion leaves and added in a little grated Parmesan cheese.'

Gerard inhaled deeply. 'The smell of garlic soda bread always takes me back to my childhood.'

'The smell of shitty nappies always takes me back to mine,' growled Una. 'Doesn't mean I like it.'

As it turned out, Una did like the garlic soda bread. For all her faults when she was wrong she admitted it, albeit grudgingly, and after eating more of the bread than anyone else, she asked Joan for the recipe.

'Would you give me a copy too, Mrs. Cahill? said Terrence. 'I'll take it back for Frances.'

'Don't bother, she won't be needing it.' As soon as the words were out of her mouth, Una realised she'd put her foot in it. 'I mean... well, if you're turning Moonbeg Manor over to An Taisce, they won't be needing a cook, will they.'

'Oh, erm... yes, of course. Well perhaps my mother could take her on.' It seemed Una wasn't the only one back-pedalling.

'Doesn't your mother already have a cook?'

'Yes, she does but Breda's getting on in years and...' Terrence had inadvertently given Una an opportunity to divert the conversation away from Frances and she wasted no time in taking full advantage.

'I'm getting on in years too, Monsignor, and so is Joan here. Are you implying that, like poor Breda, we've outgrown our usefulness?'

'No, no, not at all!' The last thing the priest wanted was to further provoke Mrs. Murphy. 'I'm sure Breda has years of service left in her. Perhaps I can find Frances a position elsewhere.'

'Perhaps Joan and I can find her something,' replied Una, sipping her tea through an enigmatic smile.

CHAPTER 24

After dinner and a generous slice of lemon drizzle cake, Gerard thanked the two women and said he had to go. He put his hand in his pocket and pulled out the mobile phone he'd confiscated earlier. He handed it to Terrence.

'Here, phone your mother.'

'I'll call her later from Mrs. Murphy's landline if it's all the same with you.' He was handing back the phone when it buzzed as a call came through. The priest instinctively reached for the answer button with his thumb and, in a flash, Gerard snatched it out of his hand.

'What in God's name are you doing? You're supposed to be dead, remember?'

'Of course. Sorry, I wasn't thinking.' Gerard shook his head in disbelief. He pulled a set of handcuffs out of his back pocket and handed them to Una.

'Thanks anyway,' she laughed, 'but I'm a bit old for kinky sex.'

'Just in case you have any trouble with our friend here. Cuff him to the radiator if you have to, but make sure he keeps a low profile.'

'You mean I can't even leave the house?' Terrence puckered his mouth into a disgruntled pout and the Inspector squeezed his eyes shut.

'I'd only just got rid of one fecking headache,' he said, through clenched teeth. 'Now I'm getting another.' Una tried to defuse the tension.

'You can take Finn out for walks,' she told the priest.

'Oh thanks,' he replied, sarcastically.

Gerard hesitated. 'I'm.... not sure that's such a good idea, Una.'

'Be grand, sure no one knows him around here. If anyone asks, he can say he's my nephew Sean from Cork.'

'Alright, but he'd better not go putting a spanner in the works after we've gone to all this trouble.'

'Is there anything to drink in the house,' asked Terrence.

'There's tea,' said Una.

'I was thinking of something stronger. If the only time I'm allowed outside this house is when your dog needs to piss or crap, I'm going to need something to numb my brain.'

Gerard took a fifty euro note out of his wallet and gave it to Una.

'Here,' he said, 'buy him a couple of bottles of whiskey. He started me smoking again and that'll probably kill me; the least I can do is help him drink himself to death.'

'Believe me, Inspector, if my mother is coming to visit, death seems like an increasingly attractive option.'

Gerard ignored the priest's remark. 'Thank you again, ladies, I'll bid you both good night.' He didn't acknowledge Terrence except to say, 'Make sure he calls his mother.'

*

There were rituals to be observed in Una Murphy's house. After the dishes had been washed and put away, the two women retired to the parlour. It was almost six o'clock and their favourite game show was about to start. They watched The Chase together every weekday evening without fail. Both had a crush on the presenter, Bradley Walsh, though it was never mentioned. Una took up her usual position in the armchair by the window. After Joan had plumped up every cushion on the sofa, something she did each time prior to sitting on it, much to Una's annoyance, she settled herself at one end. Terrence followed them in and sat at the other.

Bradley Walsh read out questions to the first contestant. He threw in the occasional joke, some funny, most corny, and Una and Joan competed to see who could answer the questions. When the second player was called, Joan tried to involve Terrence.

'Do join in, Monsignor,' she said. 'I'm sure your general knowledge is better than ours.'

'I can't be bothered,' he grumbled. 'It's hardly University Challenge, is it? A child could answer these questions.' Una didn't like having her viewing choices belittled.

'Alright so, Joan and I will keep quiet during this round and you can tell us the answers.'

After Bradley had determined the second contestant's name was Gordon, that he came from County Down and that if he won enough money, he'd like to go and see the orangutans in Borneo, he asked the first question.

'What is the capital of Mongolia?'

Gordon hesitated for a second before blurting out 'Ulaanbaatar!'

'He's right,' nodded Terrence. Una frowned at him.

'I'm not sure you've grasped the rules,' she said, testily. 'You're supposed to answer before they do, otherwise how do we know you knew?'

'Of course I knew, I just didn't say it in time.' Una decided to give him the benefit of the doubt, but she had a plan. She reached for the remote control. Bradley asked the next question.

'Who directed the 1974 film Chinatown?' Una put the TV on pause.

'Well?' she said.

'Who's going to know that?' scoffed the priest. 'It's a stupid question.'

'Do you know, Joanie?'

'Roman Polanski,' declared Joan. Una restarted the programme. Sure enough, Joan was right.

'Never mind, Monsignor, you should get the next one. After all, a child could answer these questions.'

'This is boring. I'm going to take the dog for a walk.' Finn had been asleep at Una's feet but his head shot up when he heard the magic word. The priest clicked his tongue. 'Come on, boy!' The dog didn't move.

'Get his lead from the kitchen,' said Una. 'It's hanging on the back door.' Terrence disappeared and came back with the leash. When he handed it to Una, Finn stood up and wagged his tail. She clipped one end to his collar. When she handed the other end back to the priest, the dog sat down again. Una ruffled the fur on his head. 'What's the matter?' she said. 'I've never known you turn down a walk.' She pulled him up gently by his collar and, when Terrence started for the door, the dog followed somewhat reluctantly, his tail between his legs.

'Don't forget, if anyone asks you're my nephew Sean, from Cork.'

'Yes alright, I'm not a complete idiot.' The priest left through the front door, slamming it shut behind him.

'I used to think he was such a nice fellow,' said Joan. 'He seems to have changed, even in the short time I've known him.'

'I have to agree with you, pet. It's like when the script writers suddenly change the personality of your favourite soap character. One minute they're mild-mannered and honest and the next they're lying, cheating psychopaths. If you ask me, Terrence was only nice to us when he wanted something from us. Now he thinks it's in the bag, his true colours are showing through. I'll be interested to hear what his mother has to say about him.'

Una didn't have to wait long to speak to Terrence's mother. After The Chase came Emmerdale, one of two soap operas that the two friends watched religiously, and ten minutes into it the phone rang. Una went into the kitchen to take the call.

'Hello. Una Murphy speaking.'

'Ah, Mrs. Murphy, dis is Mary McCarthy.'

'I'm sorry, I.....'

'Terry's mudder.' The woman had a Cork accent thick enough to cut with a knife. 'Am I ringing at an inconvenient time?'

'Not at all, Mary. My friend and I were just watching telly.'

'Emmerdale, is it?'

'As a matter of fact, yes. Do you watch it yourself?'

'I do o'course, and Corrie!' Coronation Street was the other soap opera the two friends watched. 'C'mere, I'll call ya back after Corry. I want to find out what yer wan Tracy is up to anyway. Talk later, bye, bu-bye, byebyebyebye.'

Una grinned as she made her way back to the parlour.

'Who was it, dear?' asked Joan.

'Terrence's mother.'

'Why are you smiling? Did she tell you something amusing?'

'No, she didn't say anything much. She's calling back after Corrie. She wants to find out what Tracy Barlow's up to.'

'Mrs. McCarthy watches Coronation Street?'

'She does, and Emmerdale.'

'I must say I'm surprised. I expected her choice of viewing to be more... sophisticated.'

'I have a feeling Mary McCarthy isn't what either of us expected, pet. You wait 'til you hear the Cork accent.'

'How did she get your number?'

'I told Gerard to give it her before we left McCarthys. I knew Terrence was reluctant to talk to her and I wanted to make sure she phoned here before she heard anything about his death on the radio. Whisht now, I've missed half of Emmerdale already.'

The closing theme tune to Coronation Street was still playing when the phone rang. Una hurried back to the kitchen and answered it.

'Well, Mary!'

'It's me again,' said Mary, redundantly. 'Jayzus, did ya see Ken's face when the police told him where Tracy's been goin' every day?' She burst into laughter. 'Isn't it grand to be a fly on the wall in someone else's living room?'

'Well it's about time they finally copped on to her. The police are always portrayed as being inept on soaps, it's the same with Emmerdale.'

'Ah stop! Dey're like the Keystone Cops!' It sounded like laughter came easily to Mary McCarthy.

'Do you like crime novels, Mary?' Una was testing the waters. 'My friend Joan and I are big fans of Agatha Christie. We've read all the Miss Marple and Poirot books.'

'I don't read much to be honest wit ya, but I've seen them on telly. Me favourite Miss Marple is Margaret Rudderford.'

'Ah, now you've said it! She's our favourite too. I've a box set of them all. The three of us should spend a day drinking tea and watching them.'

'Is dat an invitation?'

'You'd be as welcome as the flowers in May, Mary. You should stay overnight. I have a couple rooms spare now that my granddaughter is away at university.'

'Would dat be Aine?'

'Yes, how do you....?'

'I've heard all about her from Terry. My son's smitten wit yer granddaughter. Is he wit you?'

'Terrence is staying here for a while, yes, but if he doesn't stop acting like an overindulged brat, he'll find himself sleeping in the shed.' As soon as she said it, Una realised that if Terrence was overindulged, it was probably Mary who had spoiled him. She winced at her tactless remark.

'Terry? But sure Terry's a pure dote, God love him.'

Una was confused. 'I didn't think you and Terrence got along.'

Mary laughed. 'Who told you dat? I couldn't ask fer a better son. It's Stephen who's the troublemaker.'

'Stephen? Who's Stephen?'

'Terry's brudder.'

Every muscle in Una's body stiffened and, for a moment, she thought her heart would stop beating.

'Terrence has a brother?'

'Didn't he tell ya? Stephen's ten months younger.' She laughed again. 'Irish twins!'

Una had a heavy feeling in the pit of her stomach. In one fell swoop, everything she thought to be real and true had toppled down around her ears. She tried to stop her voice from shaking.

'Do they... look alike?'

'Dey're the spit of one anudder, sure nobody can tell 'em apart except me. There's somet'n in the eyes, a mudder knows.'

'Tell me about your sons.'

'Well, I don't know what to say. Terry was always a good lad. He wanted to be a priest ever since he was knee-high. Soon as he was old enough, he volunteered to be an altar boy, loved bein' in church. Stephen, ah sure he was a different kettle o' fish altogedder. Said dere was no God and we all had to help ourselves to whatever we wanted out o' life.'

'And what did he want?'

'Money! Sure dat's all Stephen ever cared about. He wanted to be rich and live the high life. Even at school, he'd t'ink up schemes to swindle his classmates outta money. Got expelled from two schools fer it! Thomas, dat's me late husband God rest his soul, he was too soft wit Stephen. He said boys will be boys and he'd grow out of it. He didn't, he just got worse as he got older. I tried to keep him in check but ahhh... the more I tried, the more he resented me. Said I was an interfering auld biddy, told me I was common as muck and should mind me own business.'

'He called you common?'

'To me face! Me Da was a fishmonger, ya see. My Tommy didn't care about dat but I was an embarrassment to Stephen. He wouldn't bring any of his friends round, not dat he had many. Said he was ashamed o' me.' Mary's voice broke slightly. She cleared her throat and carried on.

'He idolised Geraldine o'course, pretentious aul' witch. Said he wished she'd been his mudder instead o' me. She spoilt him, dat's why, gave him everyt'ing he wanted. He was like the son she never had. Two peas in a pod dey were 'til he swindled her out of a couple o' tousand punts. She wanted nutt'n to do with him after dat. She wouldn't have him at Moonbeg anymore, wouldn't even have his name mentioned. She cut him out of her will too.'

'Where's Stephen now?'

'Haven't a clue. We haven't heard from him in years.'

'The way he's going, it sounds like he'll get himself into trouble sooner or later.'

'He already did! He was banged up in prison fer... what did dey call it now? Securities fraud. He conned a group o' rich Germans into buying worthless stocks. Served t'ree years in a Berlin prison. Came out in 2008 and we've heard nutt'n from him since, not a dicky-bird. He rings Terry once in a blue moon. Last time, Stephen told him he'd got somet'n big planned.'

Una felt her skin tingle. 'Did he say what it was?'

'No. Terry told him he didn't want to know, I don't blame him.'

'Can you get in touch with Terry?'

'Well he's with the Archbishop but he'll take a call from me, why?'

'C'mere, Mary, there's no other way to put this so I'll just say it. I think it's Stephen who's staying with me.'

Mary was confused. 'But I t'ought you said it was Terry.'

'I thought it was him. Listen, this is all too complicated to go into on the phone and I know I have no right to ask you to trust me, but that's exactly what I am asking. Now you're going to hear on the news today that Terry is dead.'

'WHAT?'

'Please don't worry. We've had to stage his death to find out who murdered Geraldine. Terrence is alive and well, for now at least.'

'What do ya mean, fer now?'

'I think his life might be in danger. I want you to get hold of him on the phone and tell him to call me on this number immediately. I must speak to him.'

'Alright, but....'

'Thanks, Mary, and try not to worry. I'll be in touch.'

She ended the call, leaving poor Mary listening to a dial tone. Una shook her head. She was furious with herself. Joan's voice came floating through from the parlour.

'What's happened, dear?'

'Brace yourself, Joanie!' yelled back Una. 'You'll never believe what I'm about to tell you!'

CHAPTER 25

Una joined Joan in the parlour. 'I'm such an eejit!' she told her.

'Tell me something I don't know,' laughed Joan. Just then, the phone rang again.

'Come through to the kitchen, Joanie, you'll have to hear the story second hand.'

Joan followed her friend and stood beside her as she picked up the receiver. It was Terrence. He dispensed with formalities and got straight to the point.

'I just heard on the car radio that I died! What in God's name is going on?'

'Why didn't you tell us you had a brother?'

'Stephen? He's one of the skeletons we keep in that family closet I told you about, why?'

'Listen to me, Terrence. Your brother Stephen is masquerading as you.'

'But what's he got to do with anything? It can't be Stephen who died, he rang me half an hour ago.'

'How did he manage that? The police have his mobile!'

'He always carries a prepaid disposable. What's this about the police?'

'Just tell me what he wanted.'

'He told me to come to Ballyanny, said you knew who killed Aunt Geraldine. I think he said to meet him outside the church but I could barely hear him. The signal was bad and there was a dog barking in the background.'

'He asked you to come here?'

'Yes, straight away. It sounded urgent so I'm on my way. I've had to use the Archbishop's car because he borrowed mine a couple of days ago.'

'Who borrowed yours?'

'Stephen, and I realised afterwards my phone was in it so he's had that too.'

'Where are you?'

'I'm about ten minutes away. What's all this about, Una?'

'He murdered your aunt, Terrence! Stephen killed Geraldine and he's trying to frame poor Matty for it. I swallowed the whole thing, like an eejit! You're a loose end in all this. He'll have no choice but to dispose of you. Whatever you do, don't meet him anywhere alone.'

'Have you gone completely mad? Do you know how ridiculous all this sounds?'

'Ring Chief Inspector Quinn if you don't believe me. You remember him, don't you?'

'What's Quinn got to do with it?'

'Just ring him. Have you a pen?' Una had Gerard's mobile number scribbled on a pad beside the phone and she quickly read it out.

'Alright, Mrs. Murphy, I'll ring him, but these are very serious allegations you're making about my brother and if this is some sort of sick joke, I'll have you prosecuted for defamation of character.'

'Ingrate!' exclaimed Una, slamming down the phone. She turned to Joan who'd been standing open-mouthed beside her, trying to digest what she'd just heard. 'Stay here,' she told her. 'If Terrence rings back or the Inspector calls, keep them on the line. I won't be long.'

'Where are you going?'

'To get my dog!' Una dashed through into the hallway and was out the front door before Joan could ask anything else.

*

When Finn spotted Una, he strained at his leash to get to her.

'Hello, Terrence,' she said, patting the dog's head. 'Why are you standing in front of the church?'

Stephen was surprised and irritated to see the old woman. 'I always gravitate to churches,' he said. 'I find an aura of serenity about them.'

She smiled. 'I suppose being a priest must be a bit like being a homing pigeon in that respect. I'll tell you what. I'll take Finn home and then you can go inside and say a few prayers. Perhaps you could throw in an Act of Contrition for the poor sinners.' He handed her the lead and she started back towards the house.

'Do you need forgiveness, Mrs. Murphy?'

'I wasn't talking about me?' she called over her shoulder.

When she got back inside, she found Joan talking animatedly on the phone. 'Who is it?' she mouthed.

Joan was nodding and smiling. 'She's here now, Inspector. Yes, I'll pass you over.' She handed the receiver to Una.

'Gerard! Where are you?'

'I'm on my way to your house.'

'Ah thank God! How long will you be?'

'Five minutes or so.'

'Perfect.'

'Una, what's going on?'

'Terrence isn't who we thought he was! It's Stephen, his brother! He's been passing himself off as the Monsignor.'

'Well Terrence just called and asked me to confirm that. All I could tell him was that someone was planning to murder him. I don't know anything about a brother. Perhaps you'd care to fill me in!'

'I can't talk now.' Una's voice was barely a whisper. 'Stephen has just appeared at my kitchen window.' She put down the receiver as he came in.

'Who was that on the phone?' he asked, studying her face.

'Inspector Quinn. You'll be glad to hear they're about to arrest someone for the murder of your aunt.'

'Really?' He was visibly uneasy. 'Did he say who?'

'He didn't. My guess would be Matty.'

'Matty?' Stephen tried to feign shock. 'Surely you don't think Matty could be involved?'

'I think Frances is mixed up in it too.'

Stephen relaxed slightly. 'But what motive would they have to kill my aunt?'

'The Inspector didn't say.' Una could feel Stephen's eyes boring into her. It was time to play the innocent old lady card.

'I'd kill for a cuppa,' she said, cringing at her unfortunate choice of words. 'How about yourself, Terrence? We can have a slice of lemon drizzle cake with it.'

Stephen considered himself astute when it came to reading people, it's one of the reasons he was such a successful con man, but he still couldn't decide whether Una knew more than she was letting on. There was something about the old woman and her upper-class English friend that told him not to underestimate them. He decided to play it safe. He faked a yawn.

'Thanks for the offer but I'll pass. I'm going to turn in early. It's a tiring business pretending to be dead.'

He laughed, but his laugh was as fake as his yawn.

'Why don't you have a nice cup of tea before you go up? It's only half nine.' Una checked her watch and Stephen's intuition gave him a nudge.

'Are we expecting someone?'

'Not particularly but it's always open house here, isn't it, pet?' Joan nodded furiously. 'We never know when someone's going to pop in for a cuppa, do we?' Joan shook her head emphatically.

Stephen humoured her and sat down. Una poured his tea and he sipped it nervously. Logic told him they were just two harmless old ladies. Instinct told him to grab his passport and run. Before he could decide, there was a knock on the back door.

'See?' said Una, cheerily. 'People are always dropping by.' She pulled open the door to find Chief Inspector Quinn blocking the doorway. Stephen stood up, nearly knocking over his tea.

'Ah, Terrence,' said the Inspector. 'Don't stand on my account. I'm glad you're here, this will interest you.'

Stephen perched on the very edge of his chair. He tried hard to remain composed but his top lip was slick with sweat. The Inspector had a folder with him. He sat opposite Stephen and opened it.

'The toxicology report is back from Johann's lab,' he told Una. 'The poison used was botulinum.'

'I've heard of it,' she said. 'Isn't that what celebrities inject into their faces to make them look like wax dummies?'

'Yes and no. There are at least eight known strains of Clostridium botulinum. It's one of the most toxic natural substances in the world, like God's own nerve agent. The lab is still working to find out which strain it is. It could even be an unknown one.'

'If it is a new strain, they should name it after Finn. After all, he found it.' The little dog cocked his head at the mention of his name.

The Inspector laughed. 'It doesn't quite work like that, Mrs. Murphy, but here's a curious thing. They found traces of carrot in the sample. It seems the bacterium culture was grown on a medium containing the vegetable.'

'So that's why Finn sniffed it out!' exclaimed Joan. 'He smelled the carrot!'

'It's a wonder he's not dead,' said Stephen in a low, measured tone.

'If someone killed my dog,' replied Una, her tone equally measured, 'they'd have me to deal with.'

Just then there was another knock, this time on the front door.

'Get that would you, pet? It'll be our surprise guest.'

CHAPTER 26

As always when someone knocked at the door, Finn went berserk. He jumped up at Joan, impeding her progress through the hallway, and she tried to bat him away. When she returned to the kitchen, Finn was jumping up at someone else. Stephen leapt to his feet and, for a moment, time seemed to stand still in Una's kitchen. Even Finn didn't know what to make of it. The little terrier ran between the three men, sniffing one trouser leg after another.

Now that Una was looking for it, she could see a subtle difference between the two brothers, but it was almost imperceptible. It would be impossible if they weren't in the same room together. Terrence spoke first.

'What in God's name have you done, Stephen?'

Stephen began pacing the room. His expression was pained and he kept running his hand through his hair. Gerard kept a close eye on him to make sure he didn't make a run for it.

'It's your fault!' he spat. 'You left me no choice!'

'What's my fault?'

'You think you're better than me but you're just older, and that's only by ten months. Even so, you still get to inherit the family estate and what do I get? Nothing, that's what!'

'But you could have had the estate. I would have given it to you. The church supplies me with everything I need.'

Steven's face contorted in rage. 'There you go again, you sanctimonious bastard! Always the good one, always the perfect son. I don't want your charity, I want what's rightfully mine but that auld bitch Geraldine made sure I wasn't going to get it!'

'So you killed her. And you were prepared to kill me too. Ah Stephen.' The priest's voice cracked and Una could see he was on the verge of tears.

'How did you think you'd get away with it?' she asked Stephen.

'God, you people are so stupid! It was your own ludicrous plan that gave me the idea.'

'What do you mean?'

'You'd already killed him off for God's sake! Officially he was already dead. All I had to do was kill him, then replace the body in the morgue with his.'

'How did you think you'd manage that without being caught?' asked Gerard. 'Security at the morgue is tight.'

'I spent forty months in a German prison, Inspector. What do you think I was doing all that time? Sitting on my bunk twiddling my thumbs? I learned things in there you wouldn't believe. I broke into Moonbeg Manor without anyone knowing, didn't I? It took me forever to find those bloody slippers. Who in God's name put them in the housekeeper's wardrobe? Anyway, if I can break into a fortress like Moonbeg, a morgue wasn't going to present any problems.'

'But we would have found out that it was Terrence's body in the morgue.'

'And who could you have told? It would have been because of your stupid plan that he was dead. Think about it. Even if I was accused of the murder, you'd all be accessories before the fact. They'd have locked you up too.'

'Very clever,' admitted Gerard, reluctantly. Una needed to confirm what she had already guessed.

'You got the poison from Geoff Van Houten, didn't you.'

'How do you know that?'

'I called round the B&B's to see if they'd checked in a guest with a South African accent. One had. He wasn't using his own name of course. I had thought it might be Johann but when they said he was a young man, I knew it was Geoff. I also know that Geoff is Matty's son.'

Terrence spun round to face Una.

'WHAT?'

'Here,' she said, pulling a photograph out of her apron pocket, 'take a look at this. It was in Geraldine's bedside drawer like Frances said. It's Geoff's graduation photograph.'

'God Almighty! The similarity is striking!'

'I'm sorry, I know it must come as a shock. I found his Facebook page too and discovered that his Doctorate is in microbiology. That's how he was able to access toxins.'

Terrence was still trying to process Una's previous nugget of information. 'Do you know for a fact that Geoff is Matty's son? I mean, how....?'

'Greta and Johann spent a summer with their mother at Moonbeg, you met them there. It was the following year that Greta had the child. The poor craythur went off the rails and the boy was brought up by her moth.....'

'Who cares about Matty's bastard kid?' yelled Stephen. 'You've got nothing on me, it's all conjecture. You can't prove a thing!'

Una ignored his protestations. 'What I don't understand is why you didn't just go and stay with your aunt. You could have poisoned her food, it would have been much simpler.'

'Ah the auld bag knew the difference between me and Terry! She was the only one except for our mother.'

'Of course,' nodded Una. 'It makes sense now. She wouldn't have you in the house so you created that little yoke and put it in the slippers, then sent them for her birthday as if they'd come from Terrence.'

Gerard interrupted. 'And in response to your claims that we have no proof, that's true as it stands at the moment but we have the box the slippers came in. They were bought from an exclusive shop in Dublin. No doubt you paid cash to make sure there was no transaction record, but you might be surprised to know the shop has

CCTV. I have my men sifting through it now for footage of you buying them.'

'You might also be surprised to learn,' added Una, 'that super glue pulls off skin cells. You used it to glue your deadly little gizmo into Terrence's saddle when you broke into the barn. The samples they recovered are being processed.'

Joan had been silent throughout, slowly piecing it all together in her mind.

'Just think,' she said, 'if Stephen had phoned his mother before she phoned here, we might never have discovered any of this.'

'Agh!' spat Stephen. 'I might have known that auld bitch would be my downfall!'

'If you're wondering about your accomplice,' said Gerard, 'the South African police have a warrant out for the arrest of Geoff Van Houten. No doubt he'll accept a plea bargain. After all, there's still the small matter of his mother's suspicious death to be investigated.'

Una reached into her apron pocket and pulled out the handcuffs Gerard had given her. She returned them to him and the colour drained from Stephen's face as the Inspector pulled the young man's wrists behind his back.

'Stephen McCarthy, I'm arresting you on suspicion of murder. You are not obliged to say anything unless you wish to do so, but whatever you say will be taken down in writing and may be given in evidence.'

Terrence looked on, disappointment etched into his face. He felt sick. Forgiveness was at the very core of his faith and Stephen was his own brother, but he wasn't sure whether he'd ever find it in his soul to forgive him. As he watched him, he realised for the first time that the boy he'd played with as a child was gone. A stranger looked back at him, a mocking sneer on his face.

'It was the perfect crime,' he shrugged, 'then two old busybodies and a scruffy mutt showed up.'

Other books by W.A. Patterson

The Tipperary Trilogy:

- The Journeyman
- Safe Home
- The Devil's Own Luck

Thy Kingdom Come

The Mrs. Murphy Mysteries:-

- The Bog Body

Printed in Great Britain
by Amazon